PAT BALLARD

Once Upon Another Time

PEARLSONG PRESS
NASHVILLE, TN

Pearlsong Press
P.O. Box 58065
Nashville, TN 37205
http://www.pearlsong.com
http://www.pearlsongpress.com

Cover & book design by Zelda Pudding
Interior drawings by Eric Ballard

Original trade paperback ISBN 978-1-59719-085-5
Ebook ISBN 978-1-59719-086-2

ALSO BY PAT BALLARD

Adam & Evelyn | *ASAP Nanny* | *Dangerous Love* | *The Best Man*
Abigail's Revenge | *A Worthy Heir* | *His Brother's Child* | *Nobody's Perfect*
Wanted: One Groom | *Dangerous Curves Ahead: Short Stories*
10 Steps to Loving Your Body (No Matter What Size You Are)
Something to Think About: Reflections on Life, Family, Body Image &
Other Weighty Matters by the Queen of Rubenesque Romances

Library of Congress Cataloging-in-Publication Data

Names: Ballard, Pat (Patricia F.) author.
Title: Once upon another time / Pat Ballard.
Description: Nashville, TN : Pearlsong Press, [2016]
Identifiers: LCCN 2016043239 (print) | LCCN 2016050192 (ebook) |
   ISBN 9781597190855 (trade pbk. : alk. paper) | ISBN 9781597190862
   (ebook)
Subjects: | GSAFD: Love stories.
Classification: LCC PS3552.A4664 O53 2016 (print) | LCC PS3552.A4664
   (ebook) | DDC 813/.54—c23
LC record available at https://lccn.loc.gov/2016043239

FOR ALL OF THE OLDER PEOPLE IN MY FAMILY
who constantly fed me family history
and,
inadvertently,
gave me this story.

Chapter 1

CANDICE MOORE SAT BESIDE THE FRESHLY COVERED GRAVE in which she'd buried her grandmother yesterday and let the tears roll softly down her cheeks. She'd known this day would come. Had to come. After all, Grandma had hung on until she was 101 years old. But Candice still wasn't ready to say goodbye to her.

Grandma had been her only living relative since her mom and dad were killed in a plane crash twenty-two years ago, when Candice was only three years old. As far as Grandma knew, there were no more of their line of Johnstons around.

Grandma should know. She'd always been an avid keeper of the family tree. She had records of ancestors back to the 1600s and the founding of "these United States," as she used to declare. She also had photos of relatives back to the mid-1800s that she would pull out and share with Candice on every occasion she could. Candice always felt that since Grandma didn't have any living relatives to visit, she would just visit the ones that had gone on ahead by looking at their photos.

Candice also knew Grandma wanted to make sure that she, Candice, knew about her family line so she could pass it on to her children.

"Sure," she always told Grandma. "In this 'thin is in' day

and age, me and my plus-size body won't be likely to find a man who'd want to make babies!"

"Beauty comes in all sizes," Grandma, all of 110 pounds, would say. And she would point to a photo of one of her male relatives who'd had the honor of having a picture taken with Lillian Russell, the famous actress who was considered a sex symbol and "the American Beauty" at around 200 pounds in the late 1800s.

Candice would always reply, "Well that just proves that I was born at the wrong time, Grandma."

"Oh, Grandma! What am I going to do without you?" Candice whispered brokenly.

She realized that she'd been sitting here for a long while. It was time to head to the empty house that only held beautiful memories now that Grandma was gone.

Candice glanced around and realized that clouds had covered the sunshine. The graveyard looked lonely and dismal perched on the side of the hill out of view of the church, which was close but behind some trees.

In order to get to her car—actually, Grandma's car, which Candice had used more than Grandma had, and which she'd left parked in the church parking lot—Candice had to walk through the old part of the graveyard. So many times she'd come here with Grandma so Grandma could put flowers on some of the graves and visit other graves of relatives who had rested here since the early 1800s.

And now you rest with them, Grandma, Candice thought as she glanced back at the new grave further up the hill.

Adjusting her purse strap on her shoulder, Candice made her way down the path that led back to the church. She'd walked for a couple of minutes before she realized she was supposed to be on a small road that circled through the graveyard, not on a path.

She glanced around to see how she'd gotten off the road,

but didn't see a road anywhere. When she looked for her grandmother's grave, she couldn't see it, either. Instead of the old tombstones she'd just walked by, there were only a few new ones around. They had the same shape as the old tombstones, but were new, and the granite sparkled even though the sun was still behind the clouds.

Feeling her heart rate pick up, Candice walked faster. What was going on? Had she been in such deep mourning that she'd completely tripped out? She had to get to her car so she could sit down and think about this.

The grass on each side of the path was tall, and occasionally a briar would clutch at her clothes and try to hang on. Feeling panic rise inside her, she broke into a run and finally came around the little curve that would lead to her car at the church.

But there was no car. And there was no church.

She was looking across a vast pasture, dotted with cows lazily eating grass. A light trail meandered from the one she was on and faded into the distance.

She knew she was passing out as blackness engulfed her and she sank slowly to the ground.

CANDICE'S EYES OPENED GRADUALLY and were greeted by two very large cowboy boots.

Her gaze traveled slowly up the long legs on to the wide torso, and finally up to a shadowy face that peered from under a wide Western hat. The hot August Texas sun had come back out and rested directly behind the head of the cowboy, causing a halo that circled his hat and blinded her from seeing the face unhurriedly lowering toward her.

Beads of sweat started to pop out on her forehead as she became aware of the soft grass beneath her just as the cowboy slid his hand under her head to give it some support.

Now she could see the face that the sun and hat had been hiding. A handsome face with strength playing off of every angle. Sky blue eyes with lashes to die for peered from a bronze face that was decorated with a perfect mouth and cleft chin.

If she was dead and in hell and this was the devil, she was thankful for the few times she'd been a bad girl!

"Where's the church?"

"Church? What church? Lady, I don't have loco weeds on my ranch, but if I did, I'd swear you'd been eating them. Look around you. Do you see a church?"

Becoming agitated, Candice sat up and brought her attention back to the cowboy. For the first time, she took in his clothes. They were different than any she'd seen the local rodeo cowboys wear. This man's clothes had a more rugged look about them. As if they were deliberately designed to last a long time. As her eyes traveled down his body, she realized there was a pistol actually strapped to his hip in a holster. The kind of gun she'd only seen in Western movies.

"Where's your horse?" he asked.

"My horse?" Candice asked. As good as this guy looked, he sure acted dense. Maybe he was just a handsome kook who'd escaped the local drug halfway house down the road. Suddenly she felt uneasy. "Look, I was up there in the cemetery visiting my grandmother, who was buried yesterday, and when I came back down the hill to go home the church was gone, and so was my car," Candice tried to explain to the man.

"Your car?" he asked.

"Yes. My car. You know, one of those things you sit in and drive it to where you want to go!" This dude was slow!

"Lady, I don't know who you are or where you came from, but you must have had a bad lick on your head when you fell off your horse. You're not making one bit of sense. The only people buried in that cemetery are from old families, and none of them were buried yesterday. I'll take you back to my place, then go get Doc Wilson. Maybe he can help you get your thinking back on straight."

Before she knew what was happening he'd stood, helped her to her feet, and led her to his horse. Standing beside his horse, he leaned down and laced his fingers together, then looked up at her expectantly.

Remembering this from movies, Candice hesitantly placed her foot into his hands, but wasn't expecting the swiftness with which she was hoisted into the saddle. She quickly grasped the saddle horn to keep from going over the other side.

He stepped gingerly into the stirrup and lifted himself onto the saddle behind her, then slipped his arms under hers and around her so he could hold the horse's reins and guide it.

She held on to the saddle horn, trying not to let her arms touch his, but realized there was no way of not touching him as long as they were on this horse. Her back was pressed against his chest, and she could feel his breath fanning her hair.

"What's your name?" Candice asked, trying to get her mind off of the intimate position they were in. This was a stranger and a very strange situation, so she needed to keep her mind on the important things, like what is going on?

"Lucas Thornton," he replied.

Gazing at the terrain around them as the horse carried them further into the large pasture, cold apprehension began to form in the pit of her stomach. Something was very wrong. She couldn't bring herself to even think it, but she had to.

"Lucas, what year is it?" She closed her eyes in fear as she waited for his answer.

"1875," he answered. "I knew you must have had a bad knock on your head, and the fact that you don't know what year it is proves my suspicion."

Candice felt as if she might faint again, but fought the blackness off.

She had to look for her car. Maybe she'd gotten turned around when she was in the old section of the graveyard and gone down the opposite side of the hill. Surely the church and her car were around if she looked hard enough. And surely this cowboy was an actor and was joking when he'd said the year was 1875.

She'd bet he was taking her back to a movie set where a Western was being made.

"Which way is Dallas from here?" she asked.

"About ten miles behind us."

Feeling relief flood through her, Candice said, "So the mall is about five miles from here, then."

"The maul? Did you lose your maul with your car and the church? What were you doing with a maul?"

"You know, the shopping mall! It's about halfway between Dallas and the cemetery. Grandma's house is between the mall and Dallas."

Without warning his big hand gently cupped her head and pulled it back against his chest. "Just lie back and relax. We'll be at the house in about ten minutes."

SHE WAS TALKING STRANGE AGAIN, and he didn't have the heart to tell her that his ranch was the closest thing to Dallas from this direction. And she sure did have on strange clothes! Especially those strange britches. Even if the lick on her head was causing her to talk crazy, there was still something odd about her. But he liked the way his arms snugged around her curves.

APPARENTLY HE DIDN'T WANT TO hear her talk anymore, so she would just sit here and watch the scenery. Besides that, she kind of enjoyed the feel of her head on his wide shoulder and his strong arms holding her in place.

His large size and long arms made her feel like a little woman, and that wasn't a feeling she was used to having.

As the material of his shirt-sleeves brushed against her bare arms she could tell that the material was a rougher texture than most denim shirts were made from these days. She wondered where he got his clothes. Probably provided by the movie set.

Because there was one thing for sure—Candice knew he'd been fooling around when he'd told her the year was 1875. There was just no way that could be true. Was there?

But maybe he wasn't an actor on a movie set, either. Maybe he was some weird horse-riding, cowboy-dressing serial killer!

She was about to demand that he stop the horse and let her off when she saw a huge house in the distance, with a large barn and several smaller buildings. At one of the buildings several cowboys lounged around, just like they did in Western movies. So this really was a movie set.

Candice could feel herself relax. Finally, she'd be able to find a way to her car.

"We're almost to the house," Lucas said, pointing to the buildings ahead.

"Good," Candice said with a smile. He was really playing his role all the way. What a strange man he was. He was to-die-for handsome, but just strange.

Looking closely at the house they were approaching, Candice failed to see any vehicles that would be part of a movie set. In fact, she didn't see any vehicles at all. Just horses. And parked close to the front porch was a buggy with a horse still hitched to it.

They'd probably parked all the modern vehicles behind the house if they were filming part of the yard, too, Candice reasoned.

She was about to comment on this to Lucas when a cowboy who was unhitching the horse from the buggy spotted them and said, "Boss, your gramma is having another spell! Doc just got here and I was about to take care of his horse."

Chapter 2

LUCAS LEAPED FROM HIS HORSE AND TOSSED THE REINS TO the cowboy. He rushed up the steps to a wraparound porch, leaving Candice sitting on the horse with a panicky feeling about to take over. What was she supposed to do? Sit here until he came back?

The cowboy stood watching her, and must have sensed she was uncomfortable. "You need help gettin' off the horse?" he asked.

Remembering how cowboys in the movies got off a horse, Candice shook her head and said, "No, I'm fine." She managed to get her foot in the stirrup and swing her other leg over the horse and to the ground. But the horse shifted as she tried to dismount. She lost her footing and would have fallen if the cowboy hadn't quickly reached out and helped steady her.

"Thanks, and sorry," she muttered, without looking at the cowboy.

The cowboy shook his head and led the two horses toward the barn, leaving Candice standing in the yard wondering what had just happened.

She glanced around, trying to see someone with a camera. There was nothing that resembled a movie set in view.

Whoever these people were, they were really good at hiding their equipment.

She looked at the house. It looked like a genuine farmhouse from the mid-eighteen hundreds. One story, with a lot of windows and a wraparound porch. A porch swing and several wooden rocking chairs scattered around. Were the people who owned it getting paid well to let a movie be filmed here?

What should she do? She thought about trying to walk back to Dallas. She hadn't been paying that much attention to the direction Lucas had come, but it seemed like he'd walked the horse in a pretty straight line. And he'd said Dallas was ten miles behind them.

She turned to look back at the way they'd come, but all she could see was miles of pasture with cows grazing. In the very far distance she could see a tree line, but nothing else.

The sun would set soon, and she knew that at this time of the year it set right over Dallas. Maybe when it got dark she'd be able to see the lights from Dallas on the skyline. She wouldn't attempt to try and walk back this late at night, but if she could get an idea of the direction of the lights, she'd head in that direction early in the morning.

She was feeling hungry, but didn't dare just walk into the house and start looking for food. Well, not yet, anyway. She hadn't had any lunch because she was planning to visit with her grandma for a little while, then grab a bite to eat before shopping for groceries. No wonder she was hungry! She'd eaten a scrambled egg and some toast at eight o'clock this morning and hadn't had a bite since.

Deciding to wait until it got dark so she could get an idea about the Dallas skyline, Candice climbed the eight steps to the porch and sat down in a large wooden rocking chair that faced the setting sun.

Occasionally she could hear a noise coming from inside the house, but it was distant and nothing she could recognize.

Soon she tuned in to the cowboys and their bantering as they worked. She wasn't close enough to understand what they were saying, but occasionally could hear a loud guffaw from one of them. They seemed to be enjoying their work.

This must be a regular working ranch, she reasoned. *Surely a film crew wouldn't go the trouble of making a movie ranch look this realistic.*

That uneasy feeling tried to creep back up her spine, but she reasoned it away again. She'd almost convinced herself that this had to be a movie in the making when the screen door close to her opened wide and a plump woman with a wooden spoon and a large, empty cooking pan in her hands came out and started banging on the pan with the spoon, making a horrendous noise. "You lazy cowpokes, get yourselves in here. This grub will get cold in no time flat if you don't!"

Candice watched in amazement as five cowboys whooped and hollered as they made their way in her direction. Again she looked around, trying to find the cameras.

"Good Lord have mercy on my soul!" the woman screeched, very close to Candice. Then the woman screamed and ran toward the first cowboy who had made his way up the steps to the porch. "It's a ghost! She's Great Aunt Lela Johnston, the one in the picture! Make her go away!"

The woman turned to Candice and started waving her hands at her and saying, "Shoo! Shoo! Go on! Get out of here!"

"Mama Tanner, now, calm down." The cowboy tried to soothe her, all the while staring at Candice as if trying to make sure she really was real.

Relieved just to see more people around her, Candice said, "I'm not a ghost! Here, touch me." She held her hand out toward the woman, who screeched again and drew back against the cowboy.

The cowboy took Candice's hand in his and held it gently. "Mama Tanner, this is a real live woman sittin' here. She ain't no ghost. In fact, it's a real pretty woman!" He grinned, exposing a few missing teeth. "She may be dressed a little strange for these here parts, but she's real."

Mama Tanner reached out and cautiously poked one finger at Candice's hand, which still rested in the cowboy's rough and weathered palm. Apparently satisfied, she looked at Candice more closely and said, "Child, why are you sitting out here on this porch?"

By now the other cowboys had gathered around and were watching the action, staring at Candice in particular. The one who had led her horse away wasn't among the group.

That's when reality hit Candice with mind-boggling certainty. These guys smelled really rank. Like nothing Candice had ever come in contact with. It was a mixture of body odor from hardworking men mixed with horse and hay and who knew what else. This was real! Actors didn't need to smell the part of their role.

She was on the brink of blacking out again when Lucas's voice came through the screen door ahead of him.

"That's Candice," he said, walking up and putting his arm around Mama Tanner. "I found her out by the graveyard. She'd fainted from the heat and was talking out of her head. I'm sorry I didn't bring her inside when I got here, but I was worried about Gramma, so I kind of abandoned her." A sheepish grin turned one corner of his mouth up as his eyes finally fell on Candice. "Sorry," he said to her. "This is Mama Tanner. She's like a mama to me and most of these guys on the ranch.

"Mama Tanner, we need to let Doc look at her, too. She was pretty confused when I found her."

"I'm okay!" Candice hurried to reassure him. She didn't want a doctor looking at her. All she did was faint. Something that might happen again at any minute.

"Okay," Mama Tanner said, once again in charge. "You boys go on in and eat your supper. I'll take care of her. And young man," she said to Lucas, "I'll talk with you later about your manners! You don't leave a stranger sittin' outside in this heat."

After the porch cleared of smelly men Mama Tanner reached down and touched Candice's face, as if to make sure she wasn't left alone with a ghost.

For some reason that thought struck Candice as humorous, and a giggle erupted from her throat.

"Now, you come on, honey, and don't go getting hysterical on me. I'll take you to a room and get you relaxed, then I'll bring you some hot supper."

Standing to follow Mama Tanner, Candice glanced longingly in the direction of Dallas, but now reluctantly accepted the fact that there would be no lights illuminating the sky after the sun went down.

"I really need to use the bathroom, please," she said, feeling the sinking reality flood her.

Noticing the blank look that Mamma Tanner gave her, and remembering where she was, she said, "Um—I mean the outhouse," hoping Grandma had told her the correct word.

"Oh, how thoughtless of me! Of course you do, dear. How long have you been sitting on the porch?" She led Candice down the steps and toward the back of the house.

"Since right after the doctor got here, according to the cowboy who took Lucas's horse to the barn. He took the doctor's buggy at the same time."

"Well, that's been a while, for sure," Mama Tanner said, then mumbled something about how rude Lucas had been.

"He seemed truly worried about his grandmother," Candice offered. "I don't think he really meant to be rude."

"I know. He's a good boy. He'd have to be, to put up with the shenanigans that grandmother of his puts him through." Mama Tanner stopped abruptly and put her hand over her mouth. "Here I go again, blowing off steam. Please forgive me, but while I agree the woman is old and needs help getting around, she just gets worse about demanding attention. But let me just stop talking right now. I've said enough, and if you please, don't repeat a word I've said. It'll just upset Lucas. And he really doesn't need that, what with all he's doing to try and keep this ranch on solid ground."

"Your words are safe with me," Candice assured the woman as soon as she took a breath and Candice could get a word in.

As they left the main yard they came to a gate made from wood that was faded from years of standing in the Texas weather. It led into another sectioned-off area. The gate's rusty hinges squeaked as Mama Tanner opened it for them to go through, then closed it again. Just inside the gate she took up a large stick that had been propped against the fence.

"We have to keep this gate closed at all times. If not, Diablo, there, will get out and try to terrorize anyone who gets close to him." Mama Tanner pointed at a huge red rooster. At that moment the rooster sensed them and started prancing in their direction.

"He already has his sights on you. He knows you're new. You need to pay close attention to what I do, girl. If you don't and you come out here unprepared, this guy can really hurt you. See those spurs on the back of his legs?" She pointed to two long, pointed, really nasty-looking things on the back of the rooster's legs, a little above his feet. "Those things can cut you up pretty bad if he jumps on you and uses them."

Again, thanks to Grandma, she'd heard about how mean roosters could be, but she'd never actually seen chickens walking around in a yard like this. And she'd never had to carefully pick her way around little stacks of chicken droppings.

"Okay, stop and stand real still," Mama Tanner cautioned. "This big brute is really not liking you being here. Don't say anything or move. I'm going to have to remind him who's boss." She stepped away from Candice a little.

Just then the rooster jumped and tried to fly around Mama

Tanner to get to Candice. Mama Tanner drew back the stick and swung like she was trying to knock a baseball out of the field. The stick caught the chicken in the chest and dropped him to the ground, where he lay without moving.

"Did you kill him?" Candice asked, awestruck at the woman's quick action.

"No, I'm sure I just stunned him," Mama Tanner said. "But I don't care if I do kill him. I've tried to get Lucas to let me have this dang pest for Sunday dinner, but he raised him from a chick and is really attached to him."

She motioned for Candice to follow her as she eased to the other side of the chicken yard and started to open the second gate, keeping an eye on Diablo.

Just as Candice went through the gate Diablo sprang up and made a run at the fence, but Mama Tanner stepped through and slammed the gate shut.

The rooster flapped his wings and let out a loud crow, as if he'd succeeded in chasing them out of his yard.

"You just keep it up! I'll be the one standing over your featherless butt while you boil, and flapping my wings," Mama Tanner promised the cocky cock as he strutted around the yard.

"I don't think it'll be safe for you to even try to come through that chicken yard," she told Candice. "It'll take longer, but you'll need to walk around the yard to get to the toilet from now on."

"That sounds like a better plan to me," Candice agreed, almost shaking from the encounter. She'd never known that a chicken could be so mean!

Chapter 3

B Y NOW THEY'D REACHED THE CRUDE, YET WELL-BUILT, outhouse. But instead of stepping aside and letting Candice go in, Mama Tanner stopped and turned to Candice.

"What's your name, child? Other than Candice?"

"Moore," Candice said.

What would Mama Tanner do if Candice told her her grandma had been a Johnston? Grandma had married John Moore, but always thought of herself as a Johnston.

Feeling more confused by the moment at the situation, she said, "I really need to go in here." What she really needed was to find her way home!

"I'm sorry, child. Let me stop running my mouth and let you relieve yourself."

Candice opened the door to find exactly what her grandmother had described to her. It was a small building, maybe five feet square. Inside was a wooden box about the height of a modern commode, with a round hole cut in it. Easing closer, she looked into the hole and verified that the outhouse was perched over a hole in the ground that contained waste.

On the wall at the right of the toilet was a shelf large enough to hold a small stack of faded *Dallas Herald* newspapers. Obviously, these were to wipe with.

Hearing her grandmother talk about living like this as a child was a whole lot different than actually making herself sit on this thing, no matter how much she needed to go. Was a spider going to bite her on the butt when she sat down? Or were there snakes in there?

But she had to go!

So, setting her purse on the floor as close to the door as possible, hoping the floor was relatively clean, Candice did what any self-respecting twenty-first century girl would do. She climbed up on the seat and squatted down and did her job. No way was she going to sit over a dark, gaping hole!

After relieving herself, she tore off just enough paper to wipe with. Remembering something else her grandmother had said, she scrunched the paper between her hands to make it a little softer. Still, it wasn't at all like Charmin toilet paper when she used it! Living like this was a whale of a lot different than just hearing someone talk about it with loving memory.

She'd been so caught up in trying to figure out how to maneuver the whole outhouse thing that she'd forgotten about Mama Tanner standing outside waiting for her.

What picture of Great Aunt Lela Johnston had Mama Tanner been talking about, anyway? Was a picture of her great aunt hanging in this house? Candice's head was beginning to spin more with each question that came up. But she couldn't stand here inside this smelly toilet and try to come up with the answers. She'd just have to play it by ear, she thought as she stepped outside.

"Okay, come on," Mama Tanner said as soon as the door opened. "I'm not sure what's in that old bird's craw, but he's been prancing around the fence line the whole time you were in there. I'm not about to take you back through the chicken yard, so we'll have to walk around it. I don't think he can fly over the fence, but you need to stay on the side of me that's away from him, just in case."

Candice watched the rooster prance back and forth and felt cold chills run up her spine. Grandma would get a good laugh if she knew Candice was actually afraid of a chicken!

They'd almost made it around the chicken yard and were about to head for the back door. Diablo had taken every step they had. While Candice didn't look at him, Mama Tanner kept a close eye on him, scolding him all the while.

Suddenly, just as they were about to turn the corner and walk away from the chicken yard, Candice heard a noisy fluttering and a loud scream from Mama Tanner.

"Run, girl! He's flying over the fence!"

Before Candice could try to run the rooster had landed on her right shoulder and scraped one of his spurs along her arm, tearing the sleeve of her blouse and making a long scratch in her skin from her elbow up to her shoulder.

She fought and screamed to get the red monster off her. She fell to the ground as she frantically fought the attacking rooster, and thought she had him off her when she felt a painful rip on her right leg.

Candice sat up just in time to see Mama Tanner grab the rooster around the neck, hold him at arm's length as she whirled him around a couple times, and then give her wrist a quick snap. She heard the rooster's neck pop. Mama Tanner threw him to the ground, where his body continued to flop around even though his head hung at an awkward angle. Horrified, Candice scooted backward when the rooster came closer to her.

Mama Tanner grabbed it and tossed it farther away. "He can't harm you or anyone else!" she declared as she brushed the feathers off her hands.

"Y-you killed him?"

"That's right! I've told Lucas I was going to do just that if he didn't find a way to stop him from attacking folks. So now

I guess we'll have chicken and dumplings tomorrow!" A wide grin and twinkling blue eyes accompanied her statement.

"What's going on?" Lucas yelled, as he and several of the cowboys who had been eating came out the back door. He stopped when he saw the blood running down Candice's arm and leg.

Before he could say anything, Mama Tanner said, "Boy, I told you I was gonna kill that red devil, and now I've done it! See what he did to our guest? You need to pluck it and clean it, because we're having some chicken and dumplings tomorrow!"

Lucas didn't seem to even hear Mama Tanner as he leaned over and looked more closely at Candice's wounds. "Johnny, go tell Dr. Wilson not to leave yet. He needs to look at these scratches," he directed a tall, lanky cowboy.

"Scratches?" Mama Tanner said. "Them's more like sword wounds!"

Lucas was still ignoring Mama Tanner. Without even asking, he positioned himself on the side of Candice that hadn't been attacked and lifted her in his arms.

Candice was so surprised she forgot her pain. She was not a little woman, and this man had scooped her up as if she were a feather! And now he was carrying her up several back steps and into the house.

"Put her in the fifth room," Mama Tanner said, trotting along behind them.

Candice was barely aware that she was being taken down a long hallway, past a man standing in a doorway and a woman inside the room talking in a loud voice.

"It's okay, Gramma, I'll explain later," Lucas called to the woman.

Finally, he made it to a room and gently placed Candice on the bed. Mama Tanner quickly positioned some soft rags under Candice's arm and leg to protect the quilt from blood.

The man who'd been standing in the doorway quietly made

his way to the bedside.

"Candice, this is Dr. Wilson," Lucas said. "Dr. Wilson, this is Candice…" he paused and looked at Candice for her to fill in the last name.

When she didn't, Dr. Wilson said, "It's nice to meet you, Candice. Let me look at these cuts."

Mama Tanner put a pan of hot water with a soft rag in it on the bedside table, and Dr. Wilson began to clean the wounds.

Candice tried not to grimace when he got too close to the scratches, but occasionally just couldn't help it. Lucas and Mama Tanner hovered as close to the bed as they could get and still stay out of the doctor's way, but Candice wished they would just go away so she could grimace without feeling like a wuss.

Finally, Dr. Wilson said, "I know these cuts are painful and will be painful for a few days, but they aren't that deep or serious. Mama Tanner, if you'll bring me some honey, I'll make a bandage for her arm and leg. The honey will fight the infection while the wounds heal. I'll look at them tomorrow when I come back to check on Mrs. Thornton."

After Dr. Wilson had her arm and leg bandaged, he and Lucas went to Lucas's grandmother's room. Candice could hear them talking with the woman and the woman answering them in a slightly irritable-sounding voice, but she couldn't understand what was being said.

Mama Tanner startled Candice when she came back into the room carrying a wooden serving tray with food on it.

"I warmed up some stew for you and brought you a couple of biscuits. There wasn't a lot of leftovers. Them boys can go through a meal like a horde of ants at a picnic! But I hope this will hold you over until breakfast in the morning. Do you feel like sitting up and eating?"

Candice was trying to slide to the side of the bed and sit up, but the pain in her arm and leg was slowing her down.

"Wait!" Mama Tanner directed. "You just slide back here and lean up against the pillows and the bedstead."

Candice managed to get in a position in which Mama Tanner could set the tray across her lap. "Oh, that smells good," she said. She was so hungry that she was beginning to have hunger pains.

"Well, you enjoy it. When you're finished, just leave the tray down here by your feet and I'll be back to get it eventually. I have to clean up the kitchen and take care of a few chores first." And with that, the woman hustled from the room.

The food was even better than it smelled, and Candice could feel her spirits lifting as she filled her empty stomach.

As she ate, she glanced around the room. It was large, with high ceilings. The headboard of her bed was centered on the wall to the left of the door. Across the room, a round table with two chairs was placed in front of the only window. White, thin, lacy curtains moved gently with the breeze from the open window. A small bookcase stood in the corner to the right of the window. She was eager to see what kind of books it held.

A beautiful wooden wardrobe—or, as Grandma would have called it, a chifferobe—with carved flowers and claw feet stood against the wall directly across from the bed. The left side of the wardrobe was composed of drawers and the right side was a mirrored door. A chiffonier, or chest of drawers, with the same design stood beside the wardrobe. Candice looked more closely at the bedstead and realized it had the same design, so this was a set.

To the left of her bed was a washstand with a porcelain bowl and pitcher on the top shelf and a drawer on the bottom for storage. Sitting beside the washstand, closer to the bed, was a cream-colored enamel chamber pot. The pot had a lid with green trim and a wire bail with a green wooden handle that would make carrying the pot easier on the hands. She knew what it was because her grandmother had talked about using one as a child.

Oh, great! She sent a silent prayer that she wouldn't have to use it during the night.

The wallpaper had a subtle blue-gray background and was scattered with rosebush twigs with green leaves and small red roses in different stages of bloom. The colors were peaceful and reminded Candice that her grandmother's favorite flower was the red rose.

The entire room had a feminine feel to Candice. She wondered whose room this was. Or had been.

It suddenly hit Candice full-force that she was definitely in a different time.

Someone would find her car at the graveyard and report it to the Dallas police department. The police would go to Grandma's house and search for her, but after a while she'd become a cold case and they'd stop searching. Was this what had happened to other people who'd taken missing and never been found?

Was this what was going to happen to her? Would she ever get back home?

As darkness claimed the world outside the window, Candice cried herself to sleep.

Chapter 4

CANDICE SAT STRAIGHT UP IN BED, FIGHTING THE AIR AND trying to scream. Slowly, as she came awake, she realized it was still dark in the room and she must have been dreaming.

She felt hot and cold at the same time as she remembered the dream. Diablo had attacked her again and had her flat on her back while he stood on her chest and flapped his wings and crowed his victory.

Gradually her breathing slowed down and she started to relax. Maybe she'd be able to go back to sleep, at least until it got daylight.

She was about to doze off when a sharp pain shot through the rooster scratch on her leg. If the pain didn't leave, she'd take a pain pill. She knew she had a bottle in her purse.

Her purse! She'd dropped it when the rooster attacked her!

She had to find her purse before someone else found it and looked inside. Her driver's license would raise all kinds of suspicion.

She needed to go outside right now and look for her purse. But it was still too dark to see anything, and there certainly wouldn't be any porch lights to guide her way.

She glanced at the window and thought she could see the

hint of light from outside. Was it dawn? She'd go look out the window and see how light it was. Maybe she could see well enough to find her purse.

Without thinking about her wounds from the day before she swung her legs over the side of the bed, then winced in pain. But she realized her leg and arm felt better than they had last night.

She also realized that she needed to pee. Great! She was hoping she wouldn't have to use that chamber pot. If it was light enough she could go back to the outhouse, and that would give her an excuse to look for her purse.

Gradually, Candice made it to the window and pulled the curtains back. Just as she did so, a loud crowing startled a yelp from her. A huge white rooster stood on a fence post close to the house with its head back, crowing and flapping its wings with all his might.

"You're probably as happy that red devil is dead as I am," Candice said. At least now she knew why she'd had the dream about a rooster crowing.

As she looked out the window, she realized it was getting light outside. She could see a light pink tinge in the distant sky. Apparently, her room was facing the east, and the sun was coming up.

She'd slept in her clothes, but Mama Tanner had taken her shoes off and it was so dark Candice couldn't see where they were. She was sure Mama Tanner had put them under the bed, but after going around the bed a few times and feeling for them with her foot, she couldn't find them.

She couldn't go outside without her shoes, because she sure didn't want to step in chicken droppings with her bare feet. So she was going to be forced to use the chamber pot.

Finally giving in to her need to pee, she managed to get her pants down and squat low enough to use the pot. After relieving herself, she automatically glanced around for some paper to wipe with. Then she remembered where she was. There was nothing to wipe with, so she was going to have to pull her pants up while she was still damp from peeing. She only had this one pair of panties, and now they were going to smell like pee!

So she stood up and spread her legs as far apart as the pants still around her ankles would allow, and walked stiff-legged around the room for a few minutes until she felt dry. Then she pulled her pants back up.

She checked the pitcher, and was surprised to find water in it, and what appeared to be a small handmade bath cloth beside the basin. She poured a little water in the wash basin and splashed some on her face, then used the cloth to dry her face.

Too bad there wasn't a tooth brush close at hand.

Not wanting to get back in the bed, she pulled the curtain aside so she could see out the window, then sat down at the table and proceeded to watch the sky slowly get lighter and lighter until she could see the sun start to peek over the horizon.

Amazingly, the room had been quite cool during the night, although it was August and still hot. The high ceilings and open window had kept the temperature at a comfortable level.

One thing that was clear to Candice was that East Texas weather had been just as hot in the mid-eighteen hundreds as it was in the twenty-first century. She couldn't tell a bit of difference yesterday when she was on the back of that horse with Lucas.

Lucas. Why did her heartbeat speed up a little when she thought of him? She sure didn't need to be having any kind of lustful thoughts about him, because she was planning on finding a way back to the twenty-first century as soon as she could.

But he was a fine specimen of mankind! Nevertheless, he was here and she was going back to her time as soon as she could make her way back to that graveyard and look for the time portal.

No matter how well he filled out his jeans.

She watched the world come alive outside the window, and realized she was looking at an entirely different view than she'd had on the front porch. The back of the house overlooked a good-sized incline and a large creek that ran through the property. The water looked clear enough to walk across in places, yet she could see dark areas, too, indicating deeper holes. She'd ask Mama Tanner if there was a concealed place at the creek to take a bath.

She was about to look for her shoes and head outside when she heard a loud commotion outside the window. She couldn't see what was going on, but it didn't take her long to figure out it was the cowboys coming for breakfast.

Drat! She'd missed her chance. So what now? She wasn't getting back into bed. The bed was okay, but it sure wasn't her Simmons Beautyrest at home.

She found her shoes sitting against the wall close to the window, and put them on.

Now what? She had a sudden urge to look into the wardrobe and chest of drawers, but decided against it. It'd just be rude to plunder through other people's private stuff.

To heck with it! She was getting out of this room.

Quietly opening the door, she peered up and down the hallway to see if there was any activity. All the doors to the other rooms were closed, so she eased out of her room.

She remembered passing what she assumed was the living room when Lucas was carrying her to the bed yesterday. She'd just go there and wait until someone discovered her and told her what she was to do next.

A slight smile lifted the corners of her mouth as she remembered being carried by Lucas. She'd never have dreamed a man would actually be able to pick her up and carry her as far as he had. He was really strong. And it had felt so good to be in his arms.

No! She couldn't even start to go there. She had to find a way through the portal back to her time, so she couldn't afford to get attached to a man she could never be with.

Easing along, she became aware of voices and recognized the sound of the cowboys joking and laughing. Their voices were coming from the left doorway at the end of the hall, so she ducked into the room on the right.

The room was still a little dark because the sun wasn't completely up. But Candice could see the furniture and the layout of the room enough to know that she'd found the living room.

Across from where she stood was a large stone fireplace with a thick wooden mantel. As her eyes grew accustomed to the dim light, she could see a Victorian-style mahogany sofa covered with dark green velvet. Even in the dim light she could tell the fabric was a little worn and threadbare.

A mahogany rocking chair, covered with identical fabric as the couch, and a ladder back rocking chair were placed opposite the couch. The seating was arranged to take advantage of the heat from the fireplace in the wintertime.

A small table with two ladder back straight chairs sat in front of the two windows. The windows were covered with heavy green curtains that were closed. No wonder it was so dark in here.

Candice walked to the windows, pulled a corner of the heavy material aside, and looked out onto a porch. It was where she'd sat yesterday. A door led outside, but she decided not to try to open it. It might squeak or make some kind of noise, and she wasn't ready to alert anyone that she was awake. Hoping nobody would take offense, she opened the curtains so the room would have more light and she could look around.

For a moment she stared out over the pasture in the direction of the cemetery. She had to get back to that cemetery and see if she could find the portal. But she had no idea how she'd manage that. She couldn't ride a horse, and according to Lucas the cemetery was at least five miles from the house. She couldn't walk that far in this heat. But she'd find a way to go there alone.

Turning back into the room, which was much better lit now that the curtains were open, Candice looked at the fireplace and mantel a little more closely. The mantel was lined with beautifully framed pictures. She was about to go look at the pictures when she was overcome with an eerie feeling of deja vu. As if she'd been in this very room, looking at that very mantel But that was simply impossible.

As she moved closer to the mantel, the feeling grew. The photo frames even looked familiar. What was going on? Candice was about to freak out, but she had to get a better look at those photos.

As she stepped close enough to look at the faces in the photos, her knees almost gave way. Chills covered her body and a loud ringing started in her ears. She was going to pass out.

She grabbed one of the photos in particular and moved shakily to the closest chair, which turned out to be the ladder back rocking chair. She sat down and gazed at the photo. Gradually, she started to calm down a little as realization dawned on her.

The reason this room looked so familiar was because her grandmother had photos of it. She had copies of some of the photos that were on the mantel. And Grandma had a photo in a frame identical to the one Candice held in her hand. In fact, Candice had that photo in her purse. One more reason she had to find her purse.

She hadn't been in this room before, but she'd definitely seen it.

Chapter 5

"AACK!"

Startled out of her shocked discovery, Candice looked up to see Lucas pushing an old woman in a wheelchair into the room.

"It's her! It's Great Aunt Lela Johnston! I told all of you she was visiting me, but you just thought I was a crazy old lady. But here's my proof!"

"Gramma, that's not a ghost. This is the woman that I told you I found out by the cemetery. The one who was talking crazy because she'd fallen and hit her head on something."

Although, looking at the halo the light behind the window was casting around Candice, Lucas wasn't so sure Gramma wasn't right.

"Of course you found her at the cemetery! That's where ghosts come from!" Gramma insisted.

"She's not a ghost, Mrs. Thornton," Mama Tanner said, coming into the room to see what all the commotion was about. "But she is a Johnston. Or she knows them. She dropped her purse when Diablo attacked her, and all of her belongings fell out of it. She even has a picture in her purse like that very picture up there on the mantel."

The picture that Grandma had always cherished.

The picture that was taken at Great Aunt Lela's house.

Was this Great Aunt Lela's house? The house that Great Aunt Lela had inherited from Candice's third-great-grandmother, Lucy Johnston? Actually, Great Aunt Lela was Candice's third-great aunt, but Grandma had always called her Great Aunt Lela, and it was just easier for Candice to say the same thing.

Grandma had remembered coming to this house when she was a very small child, and that's why she loved this picture so much. Could it possibly be?

One thing was for sure—Candice didn't believe for a moment that her things had fallen out of her purse. Mama Tanner had gone through it, that's what. If she'd found the picture Candice had tucked into a side pocket of her purse, she knew Mama Tanner had gone through her purse. But she must not have found her driver's license, or didn't know what it was if she saw it, because she didn't mention it.

Gramma was talking again. "You must be from the New York line of Johnstons. Is that right, girl? Did you come down here to visit some of your dead relatives at the cemetery? And why do you have on men's clothes? Is that how women dress in New York?"

Candice listened in amazement. This old woman was handing her the excuse to be here that she needed. Although she didn't know there was a New York line of Johnstons. Grandma must not have known about them, either.

"Yes," Candice answered truthfully. "I was at the cemetery visiting dead relatives. And yes, this is what women are wearing in New York."

"But that doesn't explain how you got there," Lucas spoke up. "You said you didn't have a horse."

"Well, Lucas, you did say she'd hit her head. Maybe she can't remember where she tied her horse," the old woman reasoned. "But with all that New York money, maybe you came in a buggy. Do you remember driving a buggy to the graveyard?" she asked Candice.

"Well, however she got here, she's here, and if y'all don't come in here and eat breakfast, it's going to get cold," Mamma Tanner interrupted.

Candice wanted to hug her.

THE KITCHEN WAS A HUGE ROOM encompassing the cooking area and a large wooden table that would seat twelve people, with ladder back chairs around it. A cast iron wood-burning cook stove stood against the far wall. Beside the stove was a wooden sink with a hand pump that would dump water into the sink.

A long sideboard filled with breakfast food, plates, and utensils ran along one wall. Nothing fancy at all about this room. Just a place to cook and eat.

Candice was amazed at the food on the sideboard. Eggs, biscuits, bacon, and gravy. A coffee pot and cups were at one end of the sideboard. She followed the example of the others and took a plate and utensils and put a little of everything on her plate.

Fortunately, everyone seemed to forget about her and started talking about how hot it'd been lately. That gave Candice a chance to go back over everything that had happened to her since she awoke that morning.

Could it be possible that this very house had been in her grandmother's family line? If so, how did the Thorntons end up with it? And why did they have pictures of her Great Aunt Lela? How did they know her?

Every minute that passed just gave her more questions.

Suddenly a loud knocking on the front door interrupted everyone.

"That must be Doc Wilson," Lucas said, getting up to answer the door.

"Well, he's in a big hurry to get started this morning," grumbled Gramma. "What if I wanted to sleep in?"

"I think he's probably been up all night," Mama Tanner said. "This morning one of the boys said John Carney's wife had gone into labor last night. So Dr. Wilson may not have made it past their house to get back home. He'll probably need some breakfast." She went into the living room.

It wasn't long before Dr. Wilson and Mama Tanner came back into the kitchen.

"Morning, folks," Dr. Wilson said, taking his hat off and hanging it on a peg beside the back door.

"You can wash your hands there in the wash pan by the water bucket," Mama Tanner said, pointing at a bucket that looked a lot like the chamber pot in Candice's room.

Dr. Wilson took a long-handled dipper from the bucket and poured a couple of scoops of water into the pan and washed his hands. He dried them on what looked like a handmade towel that Mama Tanner handed to him.

"How are your arm and leg feeling this morning?" he asked, sitting down across the table from Candice.

Before she could answer, Gramma spoke up. "I thought you were coming back to see me, but you haven't even acknowledged I'm in the room! You're too busy checking on our young, pretty visitor." If an old woman could pout, Gramma did a very good job of trying.

"I'm sorry, Mable. I am here to see you, but your situation is an ongoing one, and this young woman got some pretty nasty scratches on her body that have a good chance of getting infected. I didn't mean to make your problem seem less. How are you doing?"

"I'm as good as I'm ever going to be, and you know blasted well that that's the truth! Ain't nothing you can do to make me any better. All you can do is keep me alive a little longer.

"So as soon as you finish eating, you check on her. I think

she's a relative of the folks me and my husband bought this house from, but Lucas said she hit her head yesterday when she fell off her horse, so who knows who she is. Hell, I think she may be a ghost! Lucas, take me to my room," she demanded.

"Feisty old bag," Mama Tanner muttered as she got up and went over to the cooking area.

Lucas obediently wheeled Gramma from the room and Mama Tanner busied herself with cleaning up the kitchen, leaving Dr. Wilson and Candice at the table alone.

Feeling suddenly uncomfortable by the way Dr. Wilson was looking at her, Candice made an excuse to leave the table.

"But child, you didn't eat very much," Mama Tanner scolded. "You need to keep your strength up after your day yesterday."

If you only knew, Candice thought. But she said, "I'm just not that hungry, so I think I'll go and busy myself." *Doing what?* she wondered.

"Candice, if you don't mind, I'll see Mrs. Thornton first, then I'd like to take a look at your scratches," Dr. Wilson said.

"Sure," she agreed reluctantly. "I'll just be in the room where I was yesterday."

As she reached the room where she'd slept, she remembered that she needed to empty her chamber pot. Surely she'd have time to do that before the doctor got finished with breakfast and Gramma.

But the pot was gone when she went to get it. "Now, who would have done that?" she muttered.

"I did," Mama Tanner said from the doorway. "We can't leave those things sitting around until the middle of the day. They'll start stinking. It's best to empty it and wash it out as soon as you get up and get dressed."

Feeling a little chastised, Candice nodded that she understood.

"I brought you a couple of dresses to wear until you can

get into Dallas and go shopping for some clothes that fit our lifestyle better than those fancy New York clothes you have on. I also brought you a few pair of bloomers, since you'll probably get tired of washing out the only pair you have.

"I keep up with the fashions a good bit when we manage to get a newspaper or a catalog, but we don't have any clothes like that around here. Where did you get those? In New York?"

"I ordered them online—I mean, from a catalog," Candice said. "I think it's a new company that's just starting up, so you may not ever have heard of them." She really wasn't lying.

"What's the name of this new company?"

"Amazon," Candice said.

"I'll have to watch for that," Mama Tanner said, looking almost excited about the prospect.

Candice watched as the woman put two dresses on the bed and gently swiped at the wrinkles in them. It dawned on Candice that this sixtyish, plump woman was still very style conscious.

"Mama Tanner, I don't want to take your pretty dresses," Candice said.

"They're not really mine," the woman said, and Candice saw a flicker of sadness cross her face. "They belonged to my daughter, Nellie, who died ten years ago when a horse ran away with the buggy she was driving. The buggy hit a tree and she died from head injuries two days later. I let most of her stuff go, but I couldn't give these two dresses up because I'd just made them for her.

"She was a beauty, for sure! And she loved her clothes. I try to keep up with the new fashions because I know she'd like some of them, and it makes me feel closer to her.

"You remind me of her a little, with your fancy clothes. So you wear these until you can get some new things, or until you decide to go back to New York. I'd just give the dresses to you, but I want to keep them."

Candice walked to the woman and put her arms around her. Mama Tanner returned the hug. For a few moments the two just stood and held each other, Candice missing the hugs of her grandmother and Mama Tanner missing the daughter she'd lost ten years ago.

"I'm so sorry for your loss," Candice said, pulling back from the hug.

"Don't you have anyone looking for you, child? Does your family know where you are?"

"No, my grandmother was the only one I had left—that I know of," Candice added, now wondering if she really did have distant relatives in New York.

"Well, why don't you just stay here with us and not go back? I could use some young help around here. And maybe you could win Lucas's heart and make him change his mind about marrying that Lambert girl that he doesn't love."

"Mama Tanner! That's quite enough!" Lucas said from the door.

Chapter 6

BEFORE CANDICE COULD TAKE TIME TO ANALYZE THE LOOK on Lucas's face, he continued, "Doc will see Candice now." Then he backed out the door to let the doctor in the room.

"I need to get busy," Mama Tanner said, and left the room.

Candice sat on the edge of the bed and Dr. Wilson pulled up a chair, close enough to look at her rooster wounds.

"How do your scratches feel?" he asked, taking Candice's arm and pushing the sleeve of her blouse up so he could remove the bandage.

"I'm surprised at how much better my arm and leg feel," Candice said. "That honey must be some powerful stuff."

"You act like you don't know much about honey as a home remedy," he said, casually taking the bandages off.

"I guess living in New York keeps me from knowing as much about these things than if I lived out here," she answered, thankful for her quick thinking.

"I thought you were from Dallas," Dr. Wilson said, continuing his work.

"Hmm. Well, I think that's the conclusion Lucas jumped to when he found me."

"He said you told him you were from Dallas when he found

you."

Uh-oh! Backed into a corner, Candice thought, frantically trying to find a way out of this.

"Candice, are you a Traveler?" Dr. Wilson asked, looking closely at the uncovered scratches.

"Yes, I traveled from New York," Candice lied, feeling guilty and thankful at the same time.

"I think these cuts and scratches are going to be fine. I don't see any signs of infection, so just leave the bandages off and let them heal. If you see any discharge or unusual redness, get Mama Tanner to put some more honey on them and bandage them back up. I'll look at them again in a couple of days when I come back to see Mrs. Thornton." He gently pulled the sleeve of her blouse down and let her pants leg fall back in place. "No, Candice, I mean are you a time traveler?"

Candice couldn't speak. How did he know? Why would he ask something like that?

As if reading her mind, he said, "Your clothes remind me of my first wife. She died thirty years ago in a fatal car accident."

"A car accident? As in an automobile?" Candice asked cautiously.

"Yes. It was a 1980 Cadillac." Sadness filled his voice as he spoke. "My precious little Lacy was also killed. She was only five years old. I was thirty years old, and I'd lost everything that meant anything to me."

Candice felt light-headed, and put both hands on the side of the bed to steady herself.

"You mean—you mean you—?"

"Yes. I'd taken some flowers to the gravesites, like I'd done for several months. But that particular day I was overcome with grief, even more so than usual. When I started to leave the cemetery I realized that my car wasn't where I had parked it and I was standing in a pasture."

Tears were flowing down Candice's face now, as she relived

the confusion she'd felt yesterday when she'd gone through the exact same experience.

"I take it by your reaction that you know what I'm talking about?" he asked.

"Yes, but how did you know just from my clothes?"

"Yesterday you had a scent about you that reminded me of my wife, Janey. I'm not sure if it was your perfume, hairspray, or soap, but there was something. Also, there's just a difference about you. Something more modern."

"Have you tried to go back?" Candice asked, hopefully.

"The day I arrived here I started walking west into the sunset, because I knew Dallas lay west of the cemetery. When I got there, you can understand the shock I felt. I had some money in my pocket, but I couldn't use it because I knew it would be different than anything those people had ever seen.

"As it happened, a young boy had just been hurt from falling off a horse, and the old doctor was out of town somewhere delivering a baby. So I stepped in and told the folks gathered around the boy that I was a doctor and I could help. I was an M.D., so that wasn't a lie.

"Thankfully, I'd had an interest in herbs and natural healing that I'd been learning about as a hobby, so I had an idea of what kind of medicines they would be using. And as it turned out, old Dr. Redmond needed some help and was only too happy to let me take up his slack. I learned by watching him, and became a good doctor for this day and time.

"He let me live in the room in the back of his office until I could afford my own place, and it didn't take me long to make enough money to buy a rundown old mare for a little of nothing.

"I think I finished killing that old mare by riding her out to that cemetery every time I had a chance. I walked every inch of that cemetery trying to find the portal to get back, but never even felt like I got close.

"And as my grieving wore down a little, I started to realize that I didn't have anything or anyone to go back to. I found myself enjoying helping these people much more than I'd enjoyed working in the big hospitals in Dallas.

"Then after I'd been here a couple of years, I met my sweet Nellie. I never thought I'd be able to love again after losing my Janey, but Nellie had a soothing way about her that made it impossible for me not to love her. We've been married 28 years and have a son and a daughter and four grandchildren. I don't ever go back to the cemetery anymore, because I've found happiness right here."

"What's taking you so long, Doc?" Gramma yelled from her room. "I thought you were going to come back and talk to me some more!"

A tired but patient smile crossed his face. "Well, duty calls. Listen, my advice to you would be to just keep mum about where you're actually from. I tried to confide in a few people when I first came here, hoping that I'd run across someone else who had traveled from another time, but people can really treat you like you're from outer space when you tell them. I did find one old woman who had come from the other time, and she and I had some long talks, but she had come here when she was just a child, so she and I didn't have that much in common, either, other than the traveling."

"Does Nellie know?" Candice asked.

"Yes, I told her. She was okay with it after the initial shock. But we haven't told the children, because we don't want to make them feel weird about themselves and who they are."

"But what if one of them travels one day? Shouldn't they know, so they wouldn't be so confused if they found themselves in another time and place?"

"Hmm. I never thought about that," he said. "I'll have to consider that, and maybe talk with Nellie. I'm not sure."

"DOC WILSON! ARE YOU STILL HERE?"

Chuckling and patting Candice on her shoulder, he picked up his bag and said, "Know you have a friend if you want to talk. I'll see you in a few days."

After he left the room, mixed emotions filled Candice. It was wonderful to know someone from her own time and place, yet so discouraging to hear him say how many times he'd tried to cross back to the other time and failed. Would that be what happened to her? But she couldn't imagine not trying to find her way home.

Candice decided to see if the dresses that Mama Tanner had brought her would fit. She spread both dresses out on the bed and stood looking down at them. Dismayed.

Both dresses had a slightly off-the-shoulder design, with a fitted bodice that dipped to a V just below the waistline. One skirt had three layers of tiered ruffles, but the material on the other skirt, even though it had a full style, lay flat with no ruffles.

The dress with the ruffled skirt was made from a soft pink checked fabric and looked delicate even with all the fullness to the skirt. The other dress had a deep purple background with tiny white flowers.

Glancing around, Candice was relieved to see there were no corsets, crinolines, or bustles to worry about. And apparently there would be no bra to worry about, since she couldn't wear her bra with the off-the-shoulder necklines of these dresses.

Suddenly feeling overcome, Candice sat down in the chair Dr. Wilson had pulled up to the bed and just stared at the dresses. What was she going to do? She had no idea how to maneuver in one of these things. She was sure she'd step on the hem and fall and break her neck. That would solve the problem of getting home, wouldn't it? But her gravestone would be marked in 1875 and her grandmother's was marked 2015. She'd be 141 years older than her grandmother! No, she'd better find a way to stay alive and make it back to her time.

She stood and was about to try to get into one of the contraptions on the bed when, after a brief knock, Mama Tanner burst into the room.

"I thought you might need help in getting your dress buttoned up in the back," she said. "Besides, I wanted to see you in them," she added with pride.

"I'm not sure they'll fit," Candice said, glancing at the top of the dresses. "I'm kind of big in the breast area."

"That's okay. With this design, everything that won't fit inside can just pour out the top," she said with a hearty laugh. "That'll sure enough get Lucas's attention!

"And you do have a good bit more up there than my Nellie had," she added. "I can't wait to see Lucas's face when he sees you."

Chapter 7

Mama Tanner had helped Candice decide on the soft pink checked dress, and laughed with glee at the cleavage and boob expansion that spilled over the neckline. Now they were in the kitchen preparing lunch, and Candice was still tugging at the upper part of the dress, trying to get it higher.

"Child, you might as well forget it," Mama Tanner said. "That dress ain't going any higher on your body than it is. You look fine. Just wait until you see the look on Lucas's face, and you'll know how fine you look."

"But Mama Tanner, I'm not trying to get Lucas's attention," Candice argued. "And I don't understand why you're so determined for me to get his attention. You said he's already promised to another woman. I'm not out to break up anyone's relationship."

"Well, when you find out the story behind this so-called engagement, you'll understand what I'm talking about when I say it needs to be broken up. But I can't discuss that right now because Lucas might walk in at any minute."

As if on cue, they heard the front door open. "That's probably him right now," Mama Tanner said, with a new gleam in her eyes.

Candice wanted to reach down and pull the apron she had on up over the top of her body, but refrained. But she turned her back to the kitchen door, so whoever was coming toward them would only see her back, and if she could manage it she wouldn't turn around until they left the room.

"Hello, Lucas," Mama Tanner beamed. "If you want to wash up, the food should be ready when you're finished."

"Looks like you've got some help," Lucas said, taking in the back of Candice and the new dress she had on.

"I do! And that reminds me that I want to talk with you about hiring Candice on for as long as she'll stay. You keep adding cowboys to the ranch, and I'm beginning to be overloaded with my work. I could use some help around here with all the chores."

Candice was surprised and overcome with relief to hear this from Mama Tanner. She'd wondered where she'd go from here and what she'd do until she found her way home.

She wanted to turn around and look at Mama Tanner, but couldn't bring herself to stop stirring the pot of food. Why was she feeling so shy about this dress? She wasn't a timid person by any means, but had always dressed rather modestly at home. And she'd tried not to ever flaunt her breasts.

Mama Tanner, noticing what Candice was doing, said, "You go ahead, Lucas, and wash your hands, and we can talk more about this while we eat."

Nodding, Lucas left the room, after another curious glance at Candice's back.

"Now, look here," Mama Tanner said, taking the spoon from Candice and turning her around. "You stop trying to hide what you have. You have to learn to use what you have! Take advantage of being a beautiful woman. You can have all the men around here eating out of your hands if you play it right."

"Mama Tanner! First, I'm not in the least beautiful. Look at me. Most men don't like their women to look like me. Most men want a thin, frail-looking woman.

"And second, I don't want men eating out of my hands. I don't want to bring attention to myself at all."

Mama Tanner looked at Candice as if she'd taken leave of her senses. "What are you talking about that men don't like a woman like you? Didn't you notice the cowboys looking at you all goggle-eyed? And I've seen Lucas casting glances at you, too. Now, you stop that nonsense and pay attention to what's going on around you."

As Candice stood and listened to Mama Tanner's scolding, Lucas walked back into the room. And stopped in his tracks.

His eyes took in Candice from her feet all the way to her face, stopping briefly on her low neckline and all that was there. Then his face turned red, and Candice saw anger in his beautiful blue eyes.

"What the hell is going on?" he ground out between clenched teeth. "Why are you dressed like a saloon girl? Is that what you are?"

"Lucas Thornton! Sit down while we put this food on the table, and try to not say a word," Mama Tanner directed. She placed a fresh-baked loaf of bread on the table and started slicing it. "Candice, ladle some food into a plate for each of us."

Candice did as instructed, but didn't look directly at Lucas, although she could feel his eyes on her the entire time. She found herself fighting off a case of the giggles. Here she was, a modern, twenty-first-century, enlightened woman, acting shy around a nineteenth-century down-home cowboy.

Finally Mama Tanner sat down, and Candice followed suit. She felt sure Mama Tanner had arranged it so Candice was sitting directly opposite of Lucas. When she looked up, his eyes were glued to her breasts, which rose even further out of the dress when she sat down, due to the tight-fitting bodice.

"Now," Mama Tanner said, trying to hide the gleam in her own eyes. "Lucas, this dress belonged to my precious Nellie. I had just made it and another one for her right before she died."

Candice saw the sadness flicker through Lucas's eyes briefly, before Mama Tanner continued. "Candice didn't have any clothes with her except what was on her back when that devil rooster attacked her yesterday. Anyway, I'm letting Candice borrow Nellie's dresses until she gets into Dallas and gets something to wear. I may even have to make her some dresses."

"Well, I sure hope you do! Mama Tanner, can you imagine what those men out there are going to do when they see how Candice is dressed? This will cause more chaos than a damn stampede. Don't you have a shawl or something that she can wear over her shoulders?"

"I'll see what I can come up with," Mama Tanner conceded, giving Candice a slight wink that Lucas couldn't see. "In the meantime, will you agree to hire Candice? She can help me and earn some money for new dresses."

"How long do you plan to stay?" Lucas asked, looking directly into Candice's eyes, trying to not let his eyes drop the slightest to see the beautiful view just below.

Think fast, Candice thought. This was a question she hadn't considered yet. "Well, when I came here, I wanted to stay awhile and do some research on my relatives who are buried in the cemetery. I don't really have any plans to hurry back." She was getting better with this lying thing all the time.

"How're you planning to do this research?" Lucas asked.

"I'll just ask questions of the older folks and go to the library," she said, hoping against hope that Dallas had a library at this point.

"ANYBODY GOING TO FEED ME TODAY?" The voice came from Gramma's room.

"I guess she's awake from her morning nap. I'll get her," Lucas said, pushing away from his half-eaten plate of food.

"That boy's a jewel, the way he takes care of that old bag," Mama Tanner murmured.

"Mama Tanner! She's his grandmother. He *should* take care of her," Candice said, suddenly missing Grandma.

"And she sure takes advantage of it," Mama Tanner said. "If she doesn't hurry up and pass on, I'm going to slip some poison into her food."

Before Candice could scold Mama Tanner again, she heard voices coming down the hall. Soon Lucas pushed the wheel-chair with the old woman into the kitchen.

"AAACK!" Gramma screeched when she saw Candice.

"Gramma, are you going to make that noise every time you see Candice?" Lucas asked, as he pushed her chair to the table in front of a plate of food Mama Tanner had just put in place.

"I forgot about her! And she looks more like Great Aunt Lela than she did earlier. She's even got the big bosoms like Great Aunt Lela had. And that auburn hair and the same green eyes! I'm telling you, I'm still not sure this isn't a young ghost of the woman."

"Was she your great aunt?" Candice asked. Surely she wasn't kin to the Thorntons! That would just add more weirdness to her situation.

"No, but my family knew the Johnstons very well. My Great Aunt Nora was friends with Great Aunt Lela, and they had a lot in common. They were both spinsters, so they remained friends. I used to come to this house with Great Aunt Nora and visit. So I just always called her Great Aunt Lela. When she grew too old to stay here alone, she sold this house to my husband and me."

Conversation moved on to other subjects, but Candice re-mained uncomfortable during the meal. Lucas kept casting glances at her, and although she refused to look back at him, she was sure his eyes wouldn't have met hers because they were on her low-cut dress. And Gramma kept staring at her as if try-ing to figure out who she was.

Candice wanted badly to excuse herself and go to her room,

but if she was going to be hired to help Mama Tanner, she needed to stick around to help clean up the kitchen.

Suddenly Lucas stopped eating and stared at his plate.

As if on cue, Mama Tanner roared with laughter. "I wondered how long it'd take you to realize what you were eating!"

Lucas glared at Mama Tanner for a few seconds. Then he, too, started laughing. Finally, when he caught his breath, he said, "You're an evil woman, Mama Tanner."

Candice had been enjoying her chicken and dumplings before remembering Mama Tanner saying she was going to make chicken and dumplings with Diablo. Suddenly her appetite was gone. "May I be excused, please? She pushed her plate aside.

"Now, child, you should be happy to eat that old devil of a rooster after what he did to you," Mama Tanner said.

"Let her go," Lucas said, gentle understanding in his voice. "She's not used to your cantankerous pranks. If she's really from New York, I'm sure she's used to more culture than she's finding here."

"Go on," Mama Tanner said to Candice. "I'll be there to talk with you later."

Even Gramma was laughing when Candice hurried from the room.

Chapter 8

CANDICE STOOD LOOKING OUT THE WINDOW OF HER ROOM and tried to will the queasiness to leave the pit of her stomach. Okay, she understood that people who grew up with this way of life thought nothing about killing their food and eating it fresh. But how could Lucas laugh and joke about eating something he'd considered a pet?

Grandma would probably laugh at her and tell her it's just the way country people live. But still—

After a brief knock, the opening of her bedroom door announced the presence of Mama Tanner.

"Are you okay?" Mama Tanner asked, with what actually sounded like concern in her voice. "I forget that you didn't grow up like us folks around here, and sometimes I can get carried away with my pranks, as Lucas calls them. I'm sorry if I made you feel bad."

Candice could tell Mama Tanner was serious. "I know I'm being a wuss, but that did take me by surprise."

"A what?"

"A wuss. You know, someone who acts cowardly." Candice realized the term probably didn't even exist in this time period. "It's just something they say in New York," she added, hoping that would be enough to assure the curious woman.

"Speaking of New York," Mama Tanner said, "Here's your purse. I put everything back in it after it fell open in the yard. But what is this? It has your picture on it and a lot of writing that doesn't make sense to me."

Candice took the offered purse, and the driver's license she'd hoped against hope that Mama Tanner wouldn't find. "This is just a card we have to use to get around with," was the first lame thought that came to her mind.

"Hmm. I've never read about anything like that. What are all the dates and odd stuff that's on there?" Mama Tanner insisted.

"Um, these are just codes that tell us when to renew the card and information about us."

"Well, they sure do things differently in New York than they do here. And they manage to keep their lives out of the news pretty good, too. It's like a different world there," Mama Tanner said, looking a little smug.

If you only knew, Candice thought, wondering about the look on the other woman's face.

"Anyway, after a little grumbling, Lucas has agreed to let you ride to town with him and look for some clothes. But he said to warn you that you'd have to ride in the wagon, because he has to bring too much stuff back to the ranch to take the buggy."

"That's fine," Candice said. *Maybe Lucas can take me by the cemetery to look for my car.*

"Oh, and Lucas said for you to wear a shawl. I think he's afraid he's going to be consumed with lust if he keeps looking at your plunging neckline," Mama Tanner said, with another one of her boisterous laughs. "Oh! I know just the shawl for you. I'll go get it right now."

Not trusting the gleam in Mama Tanner's eyes, Candice wondered what she was up to now. She'd never known anyone like Mama Tanner, but had to admit she was growing very fond of the woman even with all her little quirks.

She didn't have to wait long until Mama Tanner rushed back into the room carrying what looked like a large piece of lace. When unfolded, it was one of the most beautiful shawls Candice had ever seen. White lace with intricately woven roses all over it.

When Mama Tanner spread the shawl over Candice's shoulders, the gleam in her eyes was even brighter as she gave another laugh.

Candice looked down at the shawl, and realized the lace didn't hide any of her cleavage.

"Mama Tanner, you're not playing fair," Candice scolded. "This looks like I'm trying to be seductive."

"Well, Lucas said you had to wear a shawl, so this is a shawl. I'm just doing what he told me to do."

"But—"

"Now you just hush up and get outside. He'll be waiting for you by now, and Lucas doesn't like to have to wait, especially on a work day. He's got things to do."

Mama Tanner hurried Candice out the door, down the hallway, and to the front door, where Lucas was just pulling the horse and wagon up to the steps.

"Go on, now, and enjoy the ride," Mama Tanner said, pushing Candice outside, then quickly disappearing back inside and closing the door.

Feeling completely out of control of her life and wishing the portal door would open up right here and suck her back home, Candice just stood and watched Lucas pull the horse to a stop before directing his gaze to Candice.

She saw the moment when he realized what she had on and what Mama Tanner had done. She watched the emotions cross his face. First anger, then frustration, then a look she didn't understand, but looked a lot like approval.

He got down from the wagon and came to the bottom step.

Holding his hand up to Candice, he said, "That old bag is out to do me in. I'm sure she's watching me from the window, so I'm not going to give her the satisfaction of starting to yell at her. That's exactly what she wants. Come, let me help you into the wagon."

His work-roughened hand swallowed Candice's as she placed it into his. She was keenly aware of his eyes resting briefly on her exposed cleavage as he cleared his throat and led her to the wagon. "Yep, she's gonna do me in," Candice barely heard him mutter as they approached the wagon.

She couldn't stop the sweet feeling of satisfaction that ignited deep inside her being. She'd always wondered what it would be like to have a man look at her like Lucas had just done. Now she knew just how wonderful it felt. And the knowledge frightened her.

She didn't need any reason to want to stay in this place and time. She had to hold on to her determination to get home.

"I'm sorry Mama Tanner insisted that you ride with me to town today. This wagon isn't the most comfortable thing to ride in, but I have to take it to pick up supplies. You'd be much more comfortable in the buggy," he said, stopping at the front right side of the wagon and looking at Candice expectantly.

Knowing that he was waiting on her to get into the wagon, Candice looked around for somewhere to put her foot so she could step up into it. There was nothing. She looked back at Lucas, feeling completely inept.

"Just put your foot on the wheel axle and grab the seat of the wagon and pull yourself up," Lucas finally said, looking at Candice as if she were an alien.

Ha! If he only knew, Candice thought, as she lifted her foot to the axle, trying to avoid the grease she saw close to the wheel. Grabbing hold of the seat of the wagon, she made an attempt to pull herself up, only to realize she was stuck in thin air halfway up. Her dress was caught under her foot and she couldn't go forward. Deciding to ease back to the ground, her rear end came snug up against Lucas's midriff where, once again, she stopped.

Before she could react, his left arm reached around her waist and held her tightly while he pulled the dress out from under her foot with his right hand. Then, placing both of his big hands on her waist, he boosted her up into the wagon.

Feeling like a complete fool, Candice managed to sit down on the hard wagon seat and stare at her hands while Lucas climbed in beside her.

"Probably not many farm wagons in New York, huh?" he said, and Candice couldn't believe she heard laughter in his voice.

He was laughing at her! But she didn't find it amusing in the least. Well, until he started to cluck to the horse to make it move forward, but his cluck sounded more like a choking bullfrog and she knew he was trying to hide his laughter.

She looked at him and saw his shoulders shaking, and suddenly the situation caught up with her and she burst out laughing. That was all Lucas needed to allow a roar of laughter to explode from his chest.

Mama Tanner, watching the entire thing from the front door she'd left cracked open so she could see and hear what went on, felt joy rise in her heart as she listened to the laughter as the wagon headed down the road from the house.

It had been such a long time since she'd heard Lucas laugh. Really laugh, like he was doing now. It was music to her ears.

Chapter 9

As their laughter faded, Candice became aware of how narrow the wagon seat was and how close she and Lucas were sitting. In fact, his right thigh was pressed firmly against her left one, and as the wagon jostled them along, the movement of their legs rubbing against each other was causing Candice's pulse to escalate. Trying to appear casual, she attempted to move away from him, but the seat had her pinned in. There was nowhere to go.

"Sorry, but these seats are not very comfortable," Lucas said.

"I'm okay," Candice said, willing herself to act as if the touching and rubbing of their legs weren't bothering her.

Well, she'd better not let it bother her. She had to keep her feelings for this man at bay. There was no way she was going to stay in this time period and try to learn how to survive off the land. It might be fun to watch that stuff on television, but to live it? It just wasn't for her.

She spotted the cemetery to the left of the road, but knew instinctively that it was the opposite side of the cemetery from where she'd passed through the portal.

"Lucas, can we stop at the cemetery and let me check to see if my car is there?"

"You can see the cemetery from here, and obviously there is nothing there except a few headstones," Lucas reasoned.

"But if you'd stop and let me just look around, maybe I could get a clue as to where my car is," she all but pleaded.

"Look, I've got too much to do today. I need to get to town and pick up the supplies, and get back home before the rain gets here," he said. "And I'll have to tell Dr. Wilson that you're still talking out of your head, trying to find a car!"

"The rain?" Candice asked, ignoring his last statement and looking at the sky. "There's not a cloud in the sky, so why do you think it's going to rain?"

"Because the air feels more wet than usual, and I can smell the rain," he answered, without even glancing at the sky.

"Are you telling me this just to keep from stopping at the cemetery?" Candice asked in an accusing tone.

"No, I'm not. It will rain before dark, tonight. You just mark my word. But as soon as I have a day with a little extra time, I'll saddle you a horse and ride to the cemetery with you so you can look for this car of yours."

Having to accept his decision, all Candice could do was strain her eyes for her car as they went past the cemetery. Lucas was right. There was no sign of anything there except a few headstones.

Feeling hot and miserable and almost desperate, Candice snatched the lace shawl from her shoulders, folded it up, and placed it in her lap. Part of her agitation was this man so close to her. She was aware of everything about him. His large hands, with a sprinkling of dark hair enhancing his wrists and long fingers, his muscled thigh rubbing along hers, even his masculine scent.

"What are you doing?" Lucas asked.

"This is too hot and I'm not wearing it," Candice said, showing her belligerence. Up until now she'd tried to appease him and wear the hot thing, but she didn't see why she had to be miserable just because he couldn't control his thoughts.

"Well, should I take off my clothes just because I'm hot?" he asked in a perfectly reasonable tone.

"You can if you want to. But feel of this, Lucas," she said, holding the shawl out to him. "This lace is scratchy and it's making me hot. I feel much better with it off of me."

"Well, I don't feel better. I seem to get hotter when you don't have the shawl on," he said with a frown.

Candice found herself fighting to keep from giggling. Did he even realize what he'd said? She didn't dare respond to his remark, so they rode in silence.

Suddenly she heard horses approaching them from behind. They sounded like they were coming fast. Lucas heard them, too, and pulled the wagon closer to the edge of the narrow road, to let them pass.

But they slowed down as they got closer to Lucas and Candice. By the time they were beside the wagon their horses were walking and the two riders were leering at Candice.

"Who you got there, Lucas? You been keeping a secret from us?"

"Now, Tom, don't make a pest of yourself. Be nice, so the lady will think you have some class," the bigger, taller of the two said as he shifted his horse slightly ahead of the wagon, so Lucas had to pull up on the reins to stop the horse.

"Aw, Hank, she can tell I got class just by looking at me. Can't you, honey? Lucas, you gonna introduce us to your lady friend? She's mighty purty. And I really like the way that dress fits her."

Candice quietly unfolded the lace shawl and wrapped it back around her shoulders.

"Okay, boys, you've had your fun, now go on to wherever you were headed," Lucas said in a calm voice.

"Now, we can't go anywhere until you introduce us," the one called Hank said.

"Boys, this is Candice. She's a guest in my home," Lucas said, and it seemed to Candice that his voice had gotten even quieter.

"Hello," Candice said to the two.

"Where you from?" Tom asked.

"New York," Lucas said, before Candice had a chance to answer. "Now we're going to be on our way. It's way too hot to sit here in the sun and exchange pleasantries with you two." Lucas popped the reins to signal the horse to start walking. But Hank didn't move, so Lucas's horse didn't start forward.

During the brief commotion of the wagon trying to move forward and the horses shifting slightly, Lucas reached down to the floor of the wagon and to Candice's surprise came up with a double-barreled shotgun.

"Now, boys, surely you're not going to cause a scene, are you?" Lucas asked, pointing the shotgun at Hank, the rider who was blocking the wagon. He was obviously the leader of the two.

"Damn, Lucas! You're just being plain unfriendly. The boss ain't gonna like this one bit when he finds out."

"Well, you just trot on along and tell him how unfriendly I am. Maybe it'll change his mind about a few things," Lucas said.

"You'll be sorry about this," Tom yelled as he and Hank rode off in a cloud of dust.

Lucas sat and stared at the disappearing riders for a few minutes to make sure they were gone, before clucking to his horse and starting the wagon in motion again. But as soon as he found a place, he turned the wagon around and headed back the way they'd come.

"I don't trust those two for one second," he said, in explanation. "They're not beyond stopping up ahead and waylaying us when they think they can get the drop on me. I'm taking you back to the ranch."

"Who is 'the boss' and why will he be angry because you stood up to them?"

"Willard Williams owns the ranch that joins the Thornton ranch. He's wanted this ranch ever since he bought his about ten years ago, but Gramma wouldn't sell to him. He's started to get pushier now that Gramma's getting old and sick.

"He's buying up a lot of ranches around here from people who'll sell to him, and foreclosing on folks who won't sell to him. Some folks speculate that he wants to sell the land to developers who want to expand Dallas."

When they pulled back into the yard at the ranch, Lucas stopped the horse and came around the wagon to help Candice get down. She was already backing out of the wagon when he reached her, but he put his hands on her waist to steady her as she stepped down.

The shawl fell off her shoulders as she stepped down and turned to face him. His eyes automatically went to her breasts and lingered there before he raised them to look into her eyes. Candice was caught off guard at the intensity of his piercing blue stare. "I would have killed both of them if they'd tried to take you. And Candice, don't for one moment think they wouldn't have done something like that. Those two are as evil as men come.

"I'll have a talk with Mama Tanner later. Maybe she can find you something else to wear so you don't look like you're inviting attention."

And with that, he climbed back on the wagon and headed back toward town.

Candice stood and watched the wagon as it disappeared around the curve in the road.

What had just happened? She'd actually thought Lucas was going to kiss her there for a moment. The intensity of his look and words had her trembling. She couldn't put her feelings into words. It was as if he actually cared for her. And would have

60

killed for her?

"Well, come on in the house and tell me what happened." Mama Tanner spoke from the front porch.

Turning as if in a trance, Candice made her way up the steps.

Taking one look at Candice's face, Mama Tanner came across the porch and put a supporting arm around her shoulders and led her into the house and straight to the kitchen. "Now, sit down and let me get you a glass of water. Then you can tell me what happened."

While drinking the water, Candice tried to get her thoughts straight. Lucas's words, the look he gave her, and just the feelings she'd had, had unnerved her more than the encounter with the two cowboys.

When she couldn't stall any longer, Candice told Mama Tanner about the cowboys and the threats they'd made to Lucas. She left out what Lucas had said to her when they got back to the ranch.

"Willard Williams has been nothing but trouble for this community ever since he moved here ten years ago," Mama Tanner hissed. "And what hasn't made the situation any better is that when he first moved here his daughter had eyes for Lucas, and made her interest known.

"At first Lucas just ignored her, but she kept pushing, and I guess it was flattering to him, so he started seeing her. Well, she got it in her mind that they were going to get married, but Lucas wasn't interested in getting married. So she went crying to her daddy, telling him that Lucas had asked her to marry him and then changed his mind. Which was just a lie from hell.

"But apparently Daddy thought if they got married it'd be a sure way to get this ranch into his hands. So he started trying to persuade Lucas to marry Mary Beth. That's the daughter. I think Lucas was considering it until he caught Mary Beth in the loft of the hay barn with their ranch foreman. Lucas agreed not to tell her daddy, but he made it clear that there wouldn't be a wedding."

"So is Mary Beth still single and wanting to marry Lucas?" Candice asked.

"Yes, she's still single, because after all that happened she went a little batty, if you ask me. But her daddy can't see why that would make a difference to a man. 'She's still a mighty fine catch,' to quote him."

"But Lucas isn't interested?"

"No, but I'm really afraid that WW, as he's known around here, is going to start pushing harder on Lucas."

"Maybe if he married someone else Willard Williams would leave him alone," Gramma yelled from her bedroom.

Mama Tanner and Candice looked at each other in disbelief. Apparently, Gramma had been listening to every word they said.

Chapter 10

TWO WEEKS HAD PASSED SINCE THE FAILED ATTEMPT TO get to Dallas. Two weeks in which Candice and Lucas had avoided each other, other than at meals when Lucas couldn't come up with a reason to be working late when it came dinnertime.

They had both realized on that trip to Dallas that they were attracted to each other. And both had their own reasons for avoiding that attraction.

So a few days ago, Mama Tanner decided that she and Candice would go to Dallas to get Candice some clothes while the boys were out riding the fence line. That way, Lucas couldn't veto the trip.

They'd made it to Dallas and back with no problem, and had managed to find Candice four new dresses that fit her as if they'd been made for her. She'd also gotten some bloomers and three nightgowns.

Candice had also persuaded Mama Tanner to sew up the rip in her blouse torn by the rooster from hell. Occasionally she'd wear her clothes from home. The days she wore those clothes made her miss home even more.

Today Mama Tanner was busy sewing a new tablecloth

and napkins, and Candice was strolling around in the yard, enjoying the day. The weather had cooled down a little, and a nice breeze was blowing.

A perfect day to take a walk, Candice thought. And an idea came to her that wouldn't go away. The cemetery wasn't that far from here. On the spur of the moment, she decided to go there and see if she could find her car and the church. Surely the church was on the other side of the cemetery. Just maybe.

She'd walked for a while and still couldn't see any sign of the cemetery, so started wondering if this was a good idea or not. She probably needed to turn around and go back. Just before deciding to do so, she spotted the cemetery.

Excitement flooded her as she walked faster. She was happy she'd worn her slacks and blouse today, as she broke into a run.

Finally standing in the cemetery, Candice looked around. There were maybe fifty graves in all, so she started walking and looking at each tombstone. It was strange to see so many of the tombstones Grandma had brought her to see for as far back as she could remember. The same tombstones she'd seen with Grandma in her own time period. But Grandma's tombstone wasn't there. Neither were so many of the others that had been added along the way.

"So where did I pass through the time line?" Candice asked, trying to get a feel of where she was when she'd realized she was on a different path. She was slowly turning in circles, trying to get her directions worked out, when she spotted the horse and rider watching her.

As she stood rooted to the spot several thoughts flooded her mind, each one making her body a little weaker with fear. She didn't know this person, she was alone, a long way from the ranch. Nobody would hear her if she screamed for help, and she didn't have any way to defend herself. Where were cell phones when you needed one?

The rider looked to be in his mid-fifties, or maybe sixty, and still looked to be in good shape. As he got closer she could see that even though he was a classically handsome man, his clear blue eyes were hard and almost cruel-looking. She'd never seen eyes she thought looked cruel.

"You're on private property, aren't you?" were the first words out of his mouth. His voice was as hard as his eyes looked.

"I believe this is on the Thornton property, and I'm a guest at their house." Candice was pleased her voice didn't reveal how afraid she was. Feeling a little empowered because of that, she continued, "So maybe you're the one on private property."

Way to go, Candice. Make him angrier than he looks so he'll kill you and hide the body.

A smile almost touched his lips, but not his eyes. "Maybe for now, but it won't be long until I'll own this ranch and all the others around here. In the meantime, you might want to watch that smart mouth of yours when you're around Willard Williams. You don't want to make an enemy of a powerful man, now, do you?"

So this was the infamous Willard Williams. She'd have to look up his name in the land and deed archives when she got back home and see if he actually did buy out all the surrounding ranches.

"Do you?" he almost shouted.

Jumping at his voice, she answered, "No, I don't want to make an enemy of anyone, actually." *But if I had a rock, I'd try to land it upside your obnoxious head.*

"So what are you doing at the Thornton ranch?"

The man had just a little too much audacity to suit Candice, and he was beginning to get on her last nerve, whether she was alone or surrounded by an army. People like him stirred up her rebellious nature to the point of causing her to forget her fear and walk where angels feared to tread.

"I'm Lucas's fiancée," she said, lifting her chin in defiance.

"WHAT?" Willard Williams bellowed.

Oh, great. Now you've stirred the pot, Candice thought as she watched the man's face distort with anger.

"Well, we'll just see about that," he said with sudden calmness. "We'll just see about that." He whirled his horse and rode out of the cemetery at a hard run.

Feeling too weak to stand, Candice sank to the ground between the graves of her third-great aunts, Aunt Mary and Aunt Ula.

A loud crash of thunder sounded overhead, reminding Candice that the sun was no longer shining and rain seemed imminent. A flash of lightning ripped to the ground very close to her, and for a brief moment she saw through the portal to the other time. Her eyes landed on Grandma's grave for a millisecond. Then the portal closed.

"That's it!" she shouted, jumping up to go toward the spot.

Just as two strong arms grabbed her from behind and lifted her onto the back of a horse.

Chapter 11

"WHAT ARE YOU DOING?" CANDICE SCREAMED, AS SHE clawed and pulled at the hands that held her.

"I'm trying to save your life!" Lucas said close to her ear. "You almost got struck by lightning, and yet you were running toward the spot it struck instead of away from it. What is wrong with you? Did you truly hit your head harder than the doc thinks?"

It was my chance to go home, you big oaf! Candice mentally screamed as she slowly relaxed against Lucas's broad chest. Somehow she was almost happy he'd stopped her. She'd have to explore that thought later.

Rain had started peppering down on them, and she knew they'd be soaked to the bone by the time they got back to the ranch.

But Lucas wasn't headed toward the ranch, she soon realized. He pushed the horse through a thicket of pine trees and headed toward a small log cabin nestled in the midst of the pines and hidden from the road.

He got off the horse and reached up to help Candice down. "Let's get inside before we're soaked," he admonished, holding her hand and rushing to the cabin. He pushed the door open and they ducked inside just as a crash of thunder exploded all around them and the rain became a deluge.

The inside of the cabin was dim since there was only one window. The clouds and rain were making it even dimmer. But Candice could see that it looked relatively clean. A rock fireplace stood against the far wall, with a couple of pots hanging from an extended iron rod that could be swung over the fire if a person wanted to cook. It was very authentic looking, and she wondered if someone had actually cooked here.

A bed set along the side of one wall and actually had a quilt on it. Two straight-backed chairs were placed in front of the fireplace.

Finally her eyes made their way back to Lucas, who stood and watched her with a look in his eyes that she couldn't decipher.

"This cabin was on the place when my grandparents bought it. We don't know who it belonged to, but it's always had the appearance that it was lived in at one time.

"As a child, I loved coming here and pretending to be a pioneer. As I got older, I came here just because I liked it. Gramma gave me the furniture and quilt because she knew how much I loved being here."

Chills ran over Candice as she glanced around the small cabin again, wondering if some of her ancestors had actually lived here.

Lucas, sensing that Candice was cold, took the quilt off the bed, shook it a couple of times, and wrapped it around her. "Is the rain making you cold?" he asked, keeping his arms around her and pulling her against him.

"Candice Moore, what am I going to do about you? I don't need to be wanting you like I want you, but I can't seem to stop myself. You're not one of us country people. You're more refined and educated. You'd never be happy with this kind of life."

Raising her head from his warm chest, Candice looked up at him with more longing in her heart than she'd ever known. *Why now? Why him? Why here?* The questions bombarded her.

All Lucas saw was her sweet face turned up to him, with lips begging to be kissed. Slowly lowering his head, he gently covered her lips with his and was instantly consumed with their soft response.

The rain pounded the tin roof of the cabin and drowned out everything in the world except two people who were realizing how wonderful it felt to acknowledge their attraction for each other.

Reluctantly Lucas pulled away and gazed down at Candice. "You know this won't work, don't you? For all the reasons I mentioned before and even more," he said, with sadness filling his voice.

Oh, don't I know it, Candice thought. But said, "What other things, Lucas?"

"If I don't marry Willard Williams's daughter, he'll foreclose on this place as soon as Gramma dies. He owns the bank that holds the note on this place, so he's capable of taking everything I have. I'll be without a home if that happens."

"But if you own the place, why do you owe money to the bank?" Candice asked.

"Because in hard times when the ranch isn't supporting itself, I have to borrow money to keep everything running. A lot of small ranchers do that unless they're very wealthy. It was a great plan until Roy Slater, the former owner of the bank, died, and WW bought it. He's foreclosed on several ranches around here. It's like he wants to own everything around Dallas."

As he talked, the thunder storm gradually faded away and the sun began to pop back out, but his arms still held her close to him.

Candice needed one more kiss before she told him what she'd said to Willard Williams in the cemetery. After she confessed, Lucas might not want to ever talk with her again.

She stepped away from him enough to let the quilt drop from around her. Thinking she wanted free from his arms, he let go and started to back up, but she grabbed the front of his shirt and pulled him back, then raised her arms around his neck.

"Will you kiss me again, Lucas?" she asked, not believing she was being this forward.

Sucking in a ragged breath, he pulled her against him and took her lips in a kiss so fierce it almost took her breath away. Both of them realized it would probably be their last contact. He for one reason, she for another. He would marry another woman, and she would go home.

Hearts pounded so hard that neither of them knew whose heart they heard. Neither cared. And each realized at the same time that they loved the other person.

Again, Lucas ended the kiss first. He slowly pulled his lips from hers and rested his forehead against hers until he became aware of the hot tears flowing down her cheeks.

"Oh, my love, don't cry," he said, grasping her face with his large hands and wiping away her tears with his thumbs. "Please don't cry, my beautiful, strange visitor. You came and you brought such sunshine into my life. I don't know how I'm going to live without you."

Candice knew she had to confess to him. She had to tell him about her declaration to WW, and she had to tell him who she really was and that she wanted to go back home.

But did she really want to go back now? Go back to what? Just like Dr. Wilson, she didn't really have anything or anyone to go back to.

But she had to go back. Now, more than ever. She'd just tell Lucas the truth of who she was and where she'd come from, then she'd go back through the portal. That would free Lucas up to marry Willard Williams's daughter and save his ranch.

For Lucas's happiness, she didn't have a choice.

"Lucas, can we sit down? We need to talk," she whispered, feeling the strength seep from her legs.

Chapter 12

STILL HOLDING HER HAND, LUCAS LED CANDICE TO THE two chairs in front of the fireplace. After she sat down, he positioned the other chair facing her and asked, "What do we need to talk about?"

"I—I have a confession to make," she almost whispered. Actually, two confessions, she thought. "And I'm afraid you're going to hate me when I'm finished, and probably will want me to find another place to live."

"I seriously doubt that," he said, then encouraged her to continue.

She told him about his grandmother's suggestion that Candice and Lucas get married so Willard Williams would call off his attack. Then she told him about being in the cemetery and WW coming up on her, and that she'd lost her temper and told him she was engaged to Lucas.

"All that had just happened when the storm hit," she explained. "That's why it frightened me so much when you came up behind me and grabbed me. I thought he'd come back to attack me."

As Candice sat and waited for Lucas's reaction, she expected anything but the slow smile that spread across his face and the light in his eyes. Or his next words. "That's brilliant! And it might just work. I wish I'd thought of it.

"That is, if you'll marry me? Will you marry me, Candice? I know we haven't known each other that long, but we do have an attraction, and I've known marriages that started out with much less than that."

Was he asking her to marry him just to get out of marrying Mary Beth? Candice wondered. Or did he really want to marry her? Her excitement was building at that thought when reality hit her. If she married Lucas, she'd have to stay here. She couldn't ever go back to her real place in life. She'd be like Dr. Wilson. Could she do that? Could she spend the rest of her life trying to adapt to this life? This land?

She missed electricity and all the conveniences her world offered. She longed to be able to turn on a light and read at night, and not have to smell kerosene oil from the lamp. She missed running water. She longed to take a shower and shampoo her hair while the water cascaded around her. Or to just sit in a tub of hot water and take a bubble bath again. She longed to flush a toilet and be done with it instead of having to empty a chamber pot every morning.

"Lucas—there's so much you don't know about me," she said, wanting to tell him who she really was. But if she did, she was afraid the decision would be taken out of her hands.

"We can learn about each other as we go," he said, standing and taking her hands. "Come on, let's go and tell Gramma and Mama Tanner what a great idea this is. I can't wait to marry you!" And with that he pulled her against him and kissed her soundly, then led her from the cabin to the horse that stood outside.

Candice was about to remind him that she hadn't agreed to marry him yet when something made her hold back. That little voice inside her head told her to just take her time and make the correct decision. She knew that part of the right decision would have to be telling him the truth of who she was.

She needed to talk with Dr. Wilson and get his advice.

Within minutes Candice was mounted on the horse, Lucas riding behind her. But this time, his arms held her closely and his cheek rested against her hair.

His warm breath stirred her hair as he whispered "mine" in her ear.

The pure intimacy shot a bolt of awareness through Candice's entire being, leaving her weak with desire for this man whom she'd only known for such a short while. A man who'd been dead for decades when she was born. A man who might have a tombstone in the very cemetery where Grandma lay. This dash of cold reality halted all the thoughts of intimacy that had flooded Candice.

But as his warm hand moved up and down her arm, and as she rested against his warm chest, she knew this man was as much alive as she was. She wasn't sure how all this parallel time thing worked, but she was very sure this man wasn't dead.

As if she needed further proof, the hand that had been restlessly caressing her arm suddenly enveloped the side of her face and tilted her head up and back to him as his lips covered hers in a soft, probing kiss. This kiss was different. This kiss was branding her. Claiming her. Proclaiming that she was, indeed, his.

Feeling the tension on the reins, the horse came to a complete stop. The couple was so absorbed with each other that they didn't realize they were back on the public road, and that a horse and passerby had stopped to watch their public display of passion—until an ear-splitting scream brought them back to reality.

"You're cheating on me!" Willard Williams's daughter, Mary Beth, sat in a carriage and stared wildly at the couple on horseback. "You promised to marry me and now you're kissing this whore. You just wait until my daddy hears about this." She struck the back of the horse with the whip in her hand. As the horse bunched his hindquarters and took off, she tried to hit Lucas and Candice with the whip, but was too far away to reach them.

Candice had never seen Mary Beth before, but now she truly believed Mama Tanner when she'd said the woman was crazy.

"Candice, meet Mary Beth Williams. She'll truly make trouble for us. I suggest we get married as soon as possible so she can't force her father into putting a stop to our wedding."

Before Candice could answer, the ranch came into view. She was relieved to see Dr. Wilson's buggy sitting in front to the house.

"Poor Dr. Wilson. He's so faithful to stop by several times a week and listen to Gramma complain," Lucas said. "You go on in and see if he needs to check your rooster scratches again, and I'll take care of the horse."

He jumped from the horse and lifted Candice down. He kept his hands on her waist and pulled her close for just a moment and whispered, "We'll talk more about the wedding tonight, after everyone else goes to bed."

"GOOD," DR. WILSON SAID as he saw Candice in the hallway. "I was just finishing up with Mrs. Thornton and was hoping to check your scratches to make sure they're healing okay."

"I really need to talk with you, too," Candice said, leading the way to her room.

She took her usual place on the side of the bed, and Dr. Wilson pulled up a chair and sat in front of her.

"What's the matter?" Dr. Wilson asked.

Glancing at the open door to make sure nobody was nearby, Candice all but whispered. "There's so much I need to talk with you about, but I don't have any way to get to town without raising suspicion! Do you have any suggestions?"

Dr. Wilson was casually checking out the scratches on

her leg and arm as he said in an equally conspiratorial voice, "Hmm. This scratch on your arm looks like it may need a little extra attention. I could tell Lucas you need to come to my office tomorrow and let me give you some different ointment that I don't have with me. Tomorrow is the day I see patients in my office, so I won't be back out this way for a few days.

"Your scratches are healing beautifully and I don't think you'll have any scars, but we can use this as an excuse to have a private conversation. I don't know how to handle it any sooner."

"Thank you, Dr. Wilson. I really appreciate this. Tomorrow is wonderful."

"Okay, I'll tell Lucas on my way out. See you tomorrow."

Chapter 13

THE REST OF THE DAY WAS SURREAL TO CANDICE. SHE FELT as if she were hung between her world and this world. She found herself comparing and questioning everything.

Could she unlearn and forget about all the amenities she'd grown up with, and be content living in this world?

She'd find herself remembering the kisses she and Lucas had shared that morning in the cabin, and would be convinced that a love like he was offering would make up for all the other things she'd be missing. Then she'd have to make a trip to the outhouse, or be about to get a glass of cold water when she'd realize there was no refrigerator to get cold water out of.

Then she'd remind herself that she needed to go back home, so Lucas could go ahead and marry Mary Beth and save his ranch. At least, then, Gramma and Mama Tanner would still have their home.

But it would be so unfair to Lucas to expect him to give up his happiness just for the happiness of others.

When it came time for her to help Mama Tanner fix supper, Candice was so confused and frustrated that she kept forgetting what she was supposed to be doing.

When she dropped a couple of the utensils she was about

to place on the table, Mama Tanner had had enough. "Child, what is wrong with you?" she exclaimed. "What has you tied in such knots? Has Lucas done something to upset you?

"First you disappear this morning and nobody knows where you are, then you come back riding on the horse with Lucas! What? Just spit it out so we can get this food on the table for them hungry cowboys and the rest of us."

Lucas spoke from the doorway. "Mama Tanner, why don't I take Candice for a walk while you finish supper. Dr. Wilson thinks she may have a little infection in one of her scratches and wants to see her in his office tomorrow. That may have her a little upset."

"Well, child, why didn't you say something? I could put some more honey on it or something," Mama Tanner scolded.

"She'll be okay," Lucas insisted. "Come on, Candice, let's take a walk." He took her hand and led her from the kitchen while Mama Tanner grumbled about something going on that she hadn't been told about.

Lucas led Candice down the front steps and headed toward the barn, still holding her hand. He didn't say a word until they reached the barn and went inside, where she could see several horses in stalls looking expectantly at them.

Lucas released her hand. He walked to each horse and gave it a loving pat on the head or a gentle touch to its nose and mouth.

It became obvious to Candice that he was trying to figure out how to say something that was on his mind.

Finally, turning back to her, Lucas led her to some bales of hay and sat down, pulling her down beside him.

"I realize there are several things that could be bothering you. I don't think the scratches on your arm and leg are a problem, but if Dr. Wilson needs to put more medication on them, maybe you are worried about that.

"However, I realize that I kind of hurriedly forced the issue of marriage on you this morning, and I'm thinking that may be the problem.

"I also know that you're not from here. First you said Dallas, then you said New York, after Gramma suggested that was where you came from. And for all I know, you may want to go back to where you came from.

"So I'd really like to get to the bottom of it all before I force you into something you really don't want to do."

Some of the things Lucas said almost sounded like he knew Candice was from a different world.

"Well, I was the one who told Willard Williams I was your fiancée," Candice said. "So you're not forcing me into anything I didn't initiate." Not addressing wanting to go back to where she'd come from. "But Lucas, I really am worried about what WW is going to do if we go forward with the wedding.

"You said that as soon as your grandmother is gone, he'll foreclose on your ranch. So by the same token, won't he foreclose once he knows you don't plan to marry his daughter?"

"He won't do anything until Gramma is dead. That was in the contract when Granddad took out the first loan with the bank, long before Willard Williams was ever on the scene. Grandpa made sure that if anything happened to him, Gramma would have a place to live as long as a reasonable attempt was being made to make payments on the ranch. And for whatever reason, WW has agreed to honor that. I think it may be just to force me to do his bidding, but he promised not to make any moves until her death."

"I don't trust him, Lucas. I've looked into the eyes of evil on a few occasions, but never as evil as what I saw in his eyes. He's a force unto himself, and I think he'll make a move on your home as soon as he knows for sure that we plan to get married.

"So for that reason I can't, in all good conscience, marry you. It would be the end of your life as you know it.

"What would you do without your ranch? Where would all

your help go? Where would Mama Tanner wind up?"

"Candice, cowboys can always find jobs on another ranch. And Mama Tanner has friends in Dallas. She could live with any of them she wanted to."

"But what about Gramma? If WW decides to foreclose before she's gone, what would she do? It would break her heart to have to leave her home. She's lived here since she and your Grandpa bought the place."

"She could live with you and me, if you were okay with that."

"And where would that be? If you go to another ranch to work, you'd probably have to live in a bunkhouse, and your Gramma and I couldn't live there with you. What would you do if you weren't a ranch owner? Lucas, you have to think about these things."

"I know, Candice. But I love you and I want to marry you. I simply cannot imagine living with Mary Beth. I won't even try to imagine that. It would be a living nightmare.

"Together, we can work it out. Just trust me, Candice. If WW goes through with the foreclosure, we can find a way to make it work.

"So if that's all that's bothering you, just don't worry about it. Let me take care of you, okay?"

Candice could feel her pulse rate speed up as she gazed into his sincere blue eyes. Never had a man caused her heart to jump out of her chest just by looking at her. How could she possibly refuse this kind of love?

She loved the way he made her feel. She loved the way she looked through his eyes. He made her feel beautiful for the first time in her life.

"Please marry me, Candice. I think I've loved you since I found you lying in the hot grass and talking crazy out of that beautiful head of yours. But I also need you. I don't think I've ever needed anyone before, but I need you. My happiness depends on you. If you refuse to marry me, my life won't ever be the same.

"Can you take the responsibility of changing my life for the worse? That would be a horrible burden for you to carry around!"

Candice knew he was partly joking, but she believed he was also very, very serious. "You do drive a hard bargain, Mr. Thornton. That's more like blackmail than a proposal!"

"Whatever it takes to make you mine," he said, taking her face between his two large hands.

As his lips lowered to take hers, she knew she would at least wait until she talked to Dr. Wilson, tomorrow, before making her final decision.

Chapter 14

CANDICE STOOD ON THE FRONT PORCH AND WATCHED AS Lucas pulled the horse and buggy to a stop. She made her way down the steps. By the time she reached the buggy, Lucas was waiting to give her a hand up into the seat.

"This will be much easier to get in than the wagon was," he said, taking her hand as she made sure her dress wasn't under her shoe, put her other foot on the step, and climbed into the buggy.

"You're right," she said as Lucas climbed in on the other side. "That was much easier and a lot less awkward."

Candice noticed that the seat in the buggy wasn't any wider than the wagon seat, but a horse blanket had been folded and placed where she sat to give her a little padding. "Thanks for the extra padding," she said, sending Lucas a smile.

"The best part of this ride will be that we won't be afraid of touching each other like we were in the wagon," he said, sliding a little closer to Candice. They were touching from their hips to their knees. Then, holding the reins in one hand, he placed his arm on the back of the seat and let his fingers gently touch her shoulder. "Perfect," he said, squeezing her closer to his side.

"How will this look if someone sees us?" Candice asked,

thinking about word getting back to Willard Williams of them all snugged up in the buggy.

"I'll just tell them you're my fiancée and that will be that."

"But—" Candice started to argue.

"Shhhh. Just enjoy the ride. Enjoy the beautiful day. Smell the scent of the pine trees in the air. The breeze is cool and the sun is shining. And I'm going to Dallas with my fiancée. It's a great day to be alive!"

So Candice kept silent and tried to concentrate on the day. It was, indeed, an exceptionally beautiful day, and under different circumstances she would have been ecstatic.

It was mid-September, and it was hard for her to believe she'd been here over a month. Where would she be in another month? Married and living here with Lucas? Back to the present and living alone in Grandma's house with very few friends and basically nothing else?

She'd lain awake until the wee hours of the morning trying to figure out what to tell Dr. Wilson, and finally decided to tell him everything that was on her mind. There just wasn't any way to make it sound like anything other than what it was.

Lost in thought, she didn't realize horses were approaching until Lucas said, "Well, here goes."

Coming toward them were Willard Williams and three other riders. They stopped directly in front of the buggy, and Lucas gently tugged on the reins to stop the horse.

"Good morning, gentlemen," Lucas said, not moving his arm from the back of the seat.

"Isn't that just cozy," WW snarled. "Lucas, you can play around with that Calico Queen as much as you want to, but you promised to marry my daughter, and by damn, I'm here to let you know that you will marry her or I'll ruin you!

"You can keep your purveyor of pleasure until you get tired of her, and you don't need to even take Mary Beth to bed. I'd much rather you never touched her. But her name will be on the deed to your ranch. You need to make your mind up to that.

"And if you defy me by marrying this—this harlot, I'll foreclose on that ranch whether that old woman is dead or not.

"Come on, boys. This sight is making me sick." WW spurred his horse and rode off.

"I believe he called me everything but a whore," Candice said, glancing up at Lucas.

Nothing was moving on his body except the clenching and unclenching of his strong jaw. He hadn't moved his arm from around her shoulders, and was making no move to start the horse and buggy.

"Lucas?" Her voice was barely audible.

"I've never wanted to kill a man before," Lucas finally ground out. "But I truly wanted to put a bullet in his forehead. And I may before this is all over."

"It's okay, Lucas. Really, it is. Words can't hurt us, and you don't want to get lynched for killing a man."

"No! Nobody gets to call the woman I love names like that. I didn't start anything because I didn't want you to get caught in the gunfire, but the next time I see him, he'll either be on his knees begging for his life or he'll be dead. That'd be a big improvement to this community, anyway. Damn the day he ever came to this area!"

Finally, lifting his arm from her shoulders, he took the reins in both hands, clucked to the horse, and headed on to Dallas.

THEY'D MADE IT INTO DALLAS without further incident. Candice was amazed at the traffic on the streets. Horses pulling buggies of all sizes and shapes. Cowboys riding horses. People walking or running through the streets. She was surprised at how similar it all seemed to the Dallas she was used to. Just replace the horses and buggies with modern-day vehicles and change the way folks were dressed and it was pretty much the same.

Although the streets were dirt, Candice was amazed to see rails running down the middle and a mule pulling a streetcar. People on the streetcar were talking, reading newspapers, or just staring ahead, waiting to get to their destination.

She'd been expecting a small town like the ones she'd seen in Western movies at home, but this was not a small town.

"What's the population of Dallas?" she asked.

"I'm not sure, but it's grown a lot since the Houston and Texas Central and Texas and Pacific railroad tracks got here. It helps that they cross here in town. That's encouraged a lot of businesses to come to Dallas and set up shop. Of course, the fire in 1860 destroyed most of the business buildings on the square, but a lot of them have been rebuilt."

Before Candice could get her fill of looking at everything, Lucas dropped her off at Dr. Wilson's office, saying he had some business to attend to and would come back and get her when he'd finished.

So this is how it was done without cell phones, Candice mused as she made her way up the outside steps leading to Dr. Wilson's office, which was on the second floor of the small building. She assumed that if she finished first she'd just wait for Lucas to show up, and if he finished first he'd sit out front in the buggy until she was through.

Nobody was in the office when Candice went in, but the doctor's voice called from a back room. "Just have a seat and I'll be with you in a minute."

Candice glanced around the waiting room, surprised at how accommodating it was. A long church pew was placed along one wall, and several straight-back chairs with woven bottoms lined the other wall. A small desk was sitting at an angle in the far corner, so as to take up as little space as possible. There were a few papers on the desk, but Candice wondered who the desk was for. Surely Dr. Wilson didn't have a receptionist.

Candice's inspection was brought to a halt when Dr. Wilson came out of the back room. "Oh, Candice! I'm glad you made it in. And it's a good time, since I don't have any patients. Before we go into why you're really here, let me check your scratches, since that's the excuse we used to get you here."

After checking the rooster marks on her arm and leg, Dr. Wilson declared her almost healed and that the small scars would disappear in no time.

"Now, how can I help you?" he asked, sitting behind the desk and motioning for Candice to take the closest chair.

"I really don't know where to start, Dr. Wilson. So much has happened in the past few days that I'm reeling with confusion."

At the nod of his head indicating she should continue, Candice filled him in on the fact that she'd come face to face with Willard Williams, and how frightening that had been. She confessed to impulsively telling WW she was Lucas's fiancée. She told him she was now having strong feelings about Lucas, and had even considered staying in this time, but was afraid that she'd cause Lucas to lose his home if she kept him from marrying Mary Beth Williams.

"But if Lucas loves you and doesn't love Mary Beth, he would spend his life miserable just to keep his ranch and home," Dr. Wilson said. "Do you think that would be worth it to him?"

"I honestly don't know," Candice said. "That's why I needed to run this past you. I know you can't tell me what to do with my life or Lucas's, but there's something else I needed to tell you.

"When I was in the cemetery, after WW left, a sudden storm came up and lightning struck the ground really close to me. I was between my Aunt Mary and Aunt Ula's graves, and when the lightning struck, the portal opened and I got just a glimpse of Grandma's grave before the portal closed. So I briefly saw into the future, and I'm sure that's where the portal is. I thought you might want to know, at some point in time."

"I appreciate you sharing this with me," Dr. Wilson said, "but I'm sure that I'll live the rest of my life right here. I see no reason to even think of going back there now. But since you know where it is, you have a hard decision to make.

"Have you thought about asking Lucas to go back with you? It might be a way for him to get out of the mess he's in. I don't think his grandmother is going to live very much longer. Maybe six more months, but I doubt it'll be that long. I've been planning on talking with Lucas about this.

"I personally don't think he can get out of the bank problems he has. His grandfather borrowed against the ranch for years before he died, and Lucas has continued. That ranch has never been a good producer.

"The bank owners who'd been here before Willard Williams bought it out had been very lenient with a few of the ranchers. But as soon as WW got his hands on the bank, he started foreclosing as soon as he could find a reason. And personally, I think he created some of the reasons himself. A lot of odd circumstances happened to some of those ranchers that made them have to let their ranches go back to the bank.

"Lucas is the only one left. I've been expecting things to start happening—like a barn catching on fire. Or a fence accidentally being cut and cattle getting loose.

"Willard Williams is an evil man, and nobody can win against him, so far. He has the sheriff in his pocket, along with the only two lawyers in the area. So the working man can't win.

"I hate to be so discouraging, but maybe Lucas needs to relocate. It's not the worst thing that can happen to a person," Dr. Wilson said with a smile on his face.

Candice sat for a moment absorbing all that Dr. Wilson had said. "You know," she finally said, "I'd never thought about taking Lucas back with me. I wonder if he would go." Just the thought sent a streak of excitement through Candice.

"Well, you'll never know until you ask him, will you?"

"But what will I do if I tell him where I'm really from and he refuses to go back with me? He'll think I'm some kind of weirdo and probably won't want to be around me anymore."

"That's a chance you'll take by telling him. But it won't change your present situation much, will it?"

"No, I don't guess it will," Candice sighed. "And it'll make my decision of whether to go or stay a lot easier."

Chapter 15

L ucas was standing beside the buggy when Candice came down the stairs from Dr. Wilson's office. "What did he say?" Lucas asked, helping Candice climb into the buggy.

Candice looked down at Lucas's upturned face and felt a new surge of love for him. He was more caring and attentive than she ever thought a man would be toward her. She must have gotten lost in just studying his face and gazing into his sky-blue eyes, because he repeated his question. "What did he say about the rooster scratches?"

"Oh, he said they were almost healed and the scars would fade away in no time," Candice said quickly, trying to cover the embarrassment she felt for staring at him.

"So, no infection?"

"Not that he mentioned," she answered. *Now is the time to talk to him,* the little voice prompted.

"Hmm. Wonder why he thought that there might be yesterday, and today he says they're all healed up."

"Maybe they looked a little redder yesterday than they do today," she offered.

As he climbed into the buggy and clucked to the horses, Candice said, "Lucas, I really need to tell you something—"

"Can it wait awhile? I'm still really wound up about our encounter with WW earlier," Lucas said, putting his arm around her shoulders and pulling her as close as he could get her. "I just want to ride quietly with you and try and let my thoughts settle, if that's okay with you."

"What I need to say can wait," Candice said, leaning into his strong body and loving the fact that he was showing open affection to her as they rode down the street.

But how long could it wait? At least this would give her some time to decide how to approach the subject. *Lucas, would you like to take a long trip? Lucas, have I got a story for you! Lucas, you're not going to believe what I'm about to tell you—*

Breathing a large sigh of frustration, she lay her head on his shoulder and just tried to enjoy the moment.

Leaning over and kissing the top of her head, Lucas said, "I could get real used to this. In fact, I want to get real used to it, but I'll never get tired of it. I want to spend the rest of my life with you, Candice. I've made up my mind to that. No matter what sacrifice I have to make, I want you in my life."

Candice didn't answer him, but snuggled closer and smiled and wondered what in the world she was going to do.

They were almost to the ranch when a horse and rider traveling at top speed came around a curve and almost ran over them.

"Whoa!" Lucas shouted at the horse pulling their buggy, just as the rider pulled his horse to a sliding stop.

Candice recognized Johnny Lamb, the cowboy she'd learned was foreman of the ranch.

"Boss! Someone's cut the wire on the south side and all the cows in that pasture have gotten out. We're doing our best to round them up, but I'm heading into Dallas to see if I can find a few more fellas to help."

"Okay, good plan," Lucas said, waiting until Johnny got his horse back on the run before pushing the horse that pulled their buggy into a hard run.

Candice had ridden in a few cars with drivers who loved to go fast, but she'd never been as frightened as she was in the buggy. She expected it to turn over every time they went around a curve. One time the buggy skidded to the side, but Lucas hung on to the reins and the buggy managed to straighten up.

When they finally reached the ranch, Lucas jumped down and ran around to help Candice out of the buggy. "Tell Mama Tanner I don't know when we'll be in for supper, so just fix something that can feed a lot. I don't know how many will show up from town to help."

He quickly leaned down and kissed Candice, then was running toward the barn, leading the horse and buggy behind him.

CANDICE SAT UP UNTIL the clock on the mantle said midnight, waiting on Lucas to return. By then, she decided he and the other cowboys must be going to spend the night trying to round up the cows. A bright moon was shining, so they could probably see the cows okay.

Was this fence-cutting something WW had ordered? Was this what Dr. Wilson was alluding to?

While she'd waited, she'd come to a conclusion about her next move. First, she had to go back to the cemetery and make sure the opening was where she thought it was. She had to make sure she'd actually seen a glimpse into her time, and that it wasn't just some hallucination caused by the thunder and lightning. Then, after she'd confirmed the portal was there, she'd tell Lucas who she was and ask him if he wanted to go home with her, or if he wanted her to stay here with him.

She knew without a shadow of a doubt that she was in love with Lucas Thornton and wanted to spend her life with him, wherever it was.

HER FIRST THOUGHT as she came awake the next morning was that there was a party going on somewhere in the house.

After listening for a few moments, she knew the voices were coming from the kitchen and the cowboys must have gotten back.

And she had overslept! She was supposed to be helping Mama Tanner cook breakfast for the guys. She shouldn't have stayed up so long waiting for Lucas, she scolded herself as she quickly dressed and headed for the kitchen.

Just before she got to the kitchen door, she heard Lucas say, "No, let her sleep. The longer it takes for her to find this out, the better off she'll be."

"But Lucas, she has a right to know. She thinks y'all are gettin' married."

Candice realized most of the noise was coming from the kitchen where the cowboys were eating, but Lucas's and Mama Tanner's voices were coming from the living room.

"Tell me about what?" Candice said, walking into the living room to join the two.

"I'll go take care of the boys and you talk to her," Mama Tanner said. "Y'all can come up with something to beat this thing if you think hard enough."

"Let's take a walk," Lucas said, taking Candice's hand and leading her out the front door.

As they headed toward the barn, Candice asked, "Did you get the cows back?"

"We found the cows," Lucas said. The bitterness in his voice caused Candice to look quickly at him.

"Did you bring them home?" she asked.

"The ones that got out of the fence were all dead. Of course, the fence had been cut to let them out, but they had grazed their way onto Willard Williams's land, and someone had shot all of them."

"How many?" Shock and rage choked Candice's voice.

"There were around fifty head in that pasture, so I'm guessing fifty to fifty-five. We didn't take time to count them, but a few of them were ready to drop calves, so—" His voice trailed off as he opened the barn door to let them into a cool, hay-filled room. The sweet smell of the hay greeted them.

"Did you get the sheriff?"

"I sent a couple of the boys into town to report it, but we all know the sheriff is in WW's pocket. The sheriff and both lawyers in town."

"The only way to put a stop to WW is to try to get a Texas Ranger in here to straighten up this mess, but it's too late for that, I think." Resignation sounded clearly in Lucas's voice.

"Why do you say that?" Candice asked, sitting down on a bale of hay.

Lucas reached into his pocket and pulled out a piece of paper. "Because this note was nailed to a tree beside one of the dead cows."

Chapter 16

CANDICE TOOK THE PAPER THAT LUCAS HANDED TO HER and read the scribbled note.

Mary Beth is with child and she says you are the father. You will be at my house at noon tomorrow to discuss wedding plans. If you're not there, I'll come looking for you.

"No!" Candice all but shouted. "He can't do this to us, Lucas. I love you and I won't let her take you from me."

Suddenly Lucas's arms were around Candice, pulling her close. "That's the first time you've said you love me. Please say it again," he pleaded, looking down at her.

"I love you, Lucas Thornton. I want to spend my life with you, but we have a huge problem. I have to tell you something about me that may make you change your mind about wanting to marry me."

"Nothing can change my mind—" But before he could finish, loud voices came from the main house.

"LUCAS!" Mama Tanner screamed, as they heard footsteps running toward the barn.

Lucas ran to the door and snatched it open just as Johnny

was reaching for it from the other side. "Boss! You've got to come quick. Mama Tanner thinks your Gramma is dead!"

"Johnny, get into town and bring Dr. Wilson as fast as you can," Lucas shouted over his shoulder as he ran toward the house.

By the time Candice made it to the house, Lucas and Mama Tanner were gathered around Gramma's bed.

Mama Tanner was saying, "I realized I hadn't heard anything from her this morning, so I came to check on her and found her like this. She's cold, Lucas. She's been gone for several hours."

Lucas dropped to his knees beside the bed and rested his head on the bed beside his grandmother. Candice could see his shoulders shake as he wept.

Mama Tanner led Candice from the room and gently closed the door. "Leave him alone with her for a while. Even though he's been expecting this, it'll be hard on him, since she's the only living relative he has left, as far as he knows."

Candice and Mama Tanner went to the kitchen, made themselves a cup of hot tea, and waited on Dr. Wilson to arrive.

"Mama Tanner, what happened to Lucas's parents?" Candice asked. "Nobody has ever mentioned them. I told him about losing my parents, but he didn't mention his, and I didn't ask."

Candice saw an odd look cross Mama Tanner's face, but it was gone as quickly as it came. "His parents just disappeared one day. Nobody ever saw or heard from them after that. Speculation has it that they ran away from the ranch because his mom didn't like the ranching life. And his dad loved her so much that he'd do whatever she wanted.

"Gramma worshipped Lucas from the time he came into this world until earlier today when she drew her last breath. So again, speculation has it that his parents left him behind so he could work the ranch for Gramma and keep her happy."

"But I think you know or suspect something you're not telling me," Candice said, watching Mama Tanner's face closely.

"Some things are best just not thought about," Mama Tanner said, getting up and putting her cup on the counter. "I think I hear a buggy coming. It's probably Dr. Wilson." And she headed toward the front door.

Something very interesting is going on in Mama Tanner's mind, Candice thought, but stayed where she was sitting.

THAT AFTERNOON, several neighboring women came to help get Gramma cleaned and dressed so she could be "laid out" in the parlor for visitors to come by and see. Before the sun went down, someone from town had shown up with a coffin to put Gramma in.

The coffin was placed in the parlor and rested on the backs of two of the ladder back chairs from the kitchen. All the paintings were covered with white fabric out of respect. The furniture in the living room was rearranged along the walls, and more chairs from the dining room were brought and arranged around the walls.

By late afternoon, neighbors from all around started drifting in to pay their respects to Gramma. The women brought food and placed it in the kitchen along with what Mama Tanner and Candice had been cooking all afternoon.

Candice caught glimpses of Lucas on and off, but he was busy trying to organize everything that was happening.

When dark arrived, everything was finished. Gramma lay in the coffin looking more relaxed and at peace than Candice had ever seen her. The living room was full of people sitting and talking quietly, glancing at the coffin occasionally.

Candice leaned against the door jamb that led into the living room, watching everything that went on and thinking about how different this procedure was compared to Grandma's funeral. Grandma had been in a funeral home, where she was left alone both nights until they buried her on the third day.

Candice hated to leave her grandmother alone in that cold, sterile place when the visiting hours were over.

Mama Tanner had told Candice that several of the neighbors would spend the night and sit in the living room with Gramma.

"She's finally at peace," Lucas said as he slipped an arm around Candice's waist. "She won't have to worry about me or the ranch anymore. If I didn't have you, I'd want to be right there with her. Come on and walk with me for a while." He led her toward the back door.

A bright moon shone as they made their way toward the barn. Lucas led her to the fence and leaned against it as he looked out over the pasture where the remaining cows grazed. The moonlight enhanced the scene, making it look more like a painting than real life.

After a few moments he put his arm around Candice and pulled her closer to him.

"What are you going to do about WW now? she asked.

"I'm sure he's heard about Gramma by now, so I don't expect him to try and force the issue until she's buried," Lucas said. "I've asked Preacher Mead if he'll perform the service tomorrow afternoon. Several of the neighbors have volunteered to dig the grave in the morning.

"After the service, people will come back to the house to eat and visit until after nightfall. WW knows that's the custom in this area, so I don't expect to hear from him for a couple of days, at least.

"I have an idea that I want to run past you. If you'll still marry me, I want us to leave tomorrow night, after everyone goes home, and head to Fort Worth to get married. That's a little over thirty miles from here. What I'd like to do is leave here and travel for a few hours, just to get us out of the area in case WW does start looking for me. We can stop and sleep until morning, then start out again.

"There's no way we can get married in Dallas without WW finding out that it's going to happen and trying to stop it."

"Are you ready for the consequences this will bring?" Candice asked. She'd have to tell him about herself while they traveled. He might change his mind and come back here and marry Mary Beth.

"I'm ready to do whatever it takes to be married to you. I never thought I'd find a woman I would love like I do you. I figured I'd get married someday, but I never thought a lot about love. Just someone that I was compatible with.

"But you—you've brought an entirely new pattern of thinking to me, and now I don't want to settle for less than what I feel for you. I can't settle for less. And if I can't have you, then I'll remain single and alone for the rest of my life.

"Candice, you hold my future and my life in your hands, and I never thought I'd say that to another person on Earth after my parents disappeared."

"Speaking of your parents, you've never told me anything about them," Candice said, hoping he'd open up and tell her what Mama Tanner had told her.

"There's not anything to tell. One day my life was as perfect as an eight year old's life could be, and the next day my parents were gone. Nobody knows where they went, and I've never heard from them since.

"For a few years after they left I'd have a dream every once in a while that Mama Tanner would take me to see them. We'd go and spend a couple of hours, then come home. And sometimes I'd get to stay a few days with them. In my dreams it was a strange place. Everything looked different than it does here.

"My parents would tell me how much they loved me, then I'd have to leave with Mama Tanner. I' beg to stay, but they wouldn't let me.

"Then the next morning I'd get up and ask Mama Tanner if we went somewhere during the night and she'd just laugh at me and tell me I'd had that silly dream again."

Wondering about his dreams, Candice just said, "Dreams can be really weird sometimes. It's amazing how our brains come up with the stuff they do."

Lucas pulled her close and kissed her, then said, "I guess we'd better get some sleep. We have a funeral and a wedding to take care of."

Chapter 17

THE NEXT AFTERNOON, CANDICE FOUND HERSELF IN A walking funeral procession heading from the Thornton house to the cemetery. The coffin was leading the group in a black horse-pulled hearse. It was very reminiscent of the scenes she'd seen in Western movies, but she'd never dreamed she'd be a part of one.

Lucas, Mama Tanner and Candice followed directly behind the hearse. Many neighbors followed behind them. Candice was surprised at how many neighbors had gathered around to be a part of this funeral, bringing food, sitting up with the corpse, and offering comfort to Lucas and Mama Tanner.

Thankfully, a cool breeze kept the mourners from getting too hot during the relatively long walk. Maybe for these folks the walk wasn't as long as it had seemed to Candice when she'd ventured to the cemetery.

She'd wanted to get back to the cemetery and see if she could actually find the portal again, and was hoping that today she could get away from the group long enough to check between the graves of Aunt Ula and Aunt Mary.

Finally they reached the cemetery. After a couple of songs were sung by the group, Preacher Mead gave a brief talk, followed by another song. Then the entire group stood and watched as the coffin was lowered into the grave. When it was properly seated, Lucas was handed a shovel. He scooped up a shovelful of dirt and tossed it into the grave.

While the grave was being filled with dirt by those appointed to the task, well-wishers clustered around Lucas, shaking his hand and offering solace in any way they could.

Candice saw that Lucas was completely surrounded and that it would take a while for all the people to talk to him, so she eased away and headed for her aunts' graves.

She had mixed emotions about getting too close to the portal, because now she didn't want to go back to her time without Lucas. Of course, now that she knew where the portal was, she might be able to come back if she accidentally went through and didn't want to stay.

Very slowly and carefully she approached the two graves. About halfway between them, she saw the air in a certain spot looked hazy, with a slight shimmering to it. "It's really here," she whispered to herself, and stepped back instantly.

Looking toward the gravesite where Lucas was still busy with his neighbors, Candice's eyes caught and lingered on Mama Tanner, who stood a little removed from the rest and was closely watching Candice. But Mama Tanner quickly looked away when Candice looked at her. The interaction seemed a little strange to Candice, but she quickly forgot about it, realizing the significance of knowing she'd truly found the time portal.

At least half of the mourners came back to the house to eat and visit some more. Mama Tanner and Candice made sure the food, plates and utensils were available for anyone who wanted to eat, then Mama Tanner went to the parlor to visit. Lucas and a group of men were outside eating their food while they discussed ranching and all that went with it.

Feeling like the odd person out, Candice decided to go to her room and rest for a little while and think about how and when she was going to tell Lucas who she really was.

Thinking about the pending trip and wedding, she gathered what few items she planned to take and put them in a chair to wait and see if Lucas had some kind of trunk or something to pack them in.

Then she sat at the little table by the window, which had become one of her favorite places in the house. She could look out over the view and let her mind go free. Today she tried to think about being back in her own time period without Lucas, this house and this ranch. She knew life would be physically easier for her if she went back. She knew she'd remember this place and lifestyle and even long for it, if she left. But she just couldn't imagine life anywhere without Lucas.

But what was really best for him? He declared that he was ready to take his chances on Willard Williams, but was he, when it came down to the harm WW could cause Lucas and his ranch?

She was so mentally tired of trying to figure out what to do! Plus she was tired from all the activities of the past couple of days. She decided to lie down on the bed and rest. Her head had barely touched the pillow before she drifted into a sound sleep.

The next thing she knew a hand was on her shoulder, and she looked up to see Lucas standing beside the bed.

"Everyone's left, so you and I need to leave, too. It's almost dark, so by the time we get everything ready, it'll be dark enough that anyone watching won't be able to see us leave."

"My things are on that chair," Candice said, pointing to them. "I didn't know what I was supposed to do with them."

"I'll take care of it. Why don't you grab a bite to eat, then we'll be on our way. I've got the horse and buggy ready to go."

In the dining room, Candice saw that Mama Tanner had been busy putting everything away, and was overcome with guilt.

"I'm so sorry I didn't come down and help you clean up!" she said, wrapping her arms around Mama Tanner and giving her a big hug.

"Now, that's perfectly okay. Several of the kind neighbors helped me put stuff away. Plus, you needed to get some rest before this trip ahead of you. This is going to be hard for you. I'm sure you're not used to traveling a long way on a buggy. Not from where you came from."

Before Candice could reply, Mama Tanner handed her a plate of food and said, "Sit down and eat. Lucas ate something before he woke you up. I've packed a large basket for y'all to take with you. I think it should last until you get to Fort Worth."

"It'll be odd traveling in the dark," Candice ventured. "But I'm sure Lucas knows how to get there, so I'm not worried."

"If anyone can keep you safe, it's Lucas. I just hope he can keep himself safe. I don't trust that Willard Williams for a second. And he's going to be fit to be tied when he finds out Lucas is married. I have to admit, I thought this was a good idea when we first started talking about it, but now I'm a little worried. Not that Lucas has much of a choice. He sure can't marry that Mary Beth hussy."

"Mama Tanner!" Candice scolded, but couldn't hide the smile that forced its way out. "What do you mean by much of a choice? Is there another way around this?"

"No. You two need to get married, but I do have something I may run by you when you get back. And that's all I'm going to say about that."

And that was just as well, because Lucas came in at that moment and said everything was ready to go when Candice got finished with eating.

"I'm ready," she said. She was so excited that she couldn't eat anything, even if she'd been hungry.

Lucas carried the basket of food and put it in the buggy,

while Candice and Mama Tanner hugged goodbye.

"Now, you enjoy yourself. And be sure to tell Lucas anything about yourself that you think he needs to know. It'll be easy to talk while you're riding in the dark."

Lucas returned at that point, and Candice pondered Mama Tanner's strange words while he hugged Mama Tanner goodbye and listened to her advice.

Chapter 18

THE NIGHT WAS PITCH BLACK AS THE HORSE AND BUGGY pulled away from the ranch house. Millions of stars twinkled in the vast sky overhead, but didn't seem to lend one bit of light to the earth.

"How's the horse going to know where to walk?" Candice asked. "I can't even see the road. In fact, how do you know where we're going?"

"Well, first," Lucas said, wrapping his arm around her shoulder and pulling her closer, as if to reassure her, "horses can see better at night than we can. And second, I've traveled these roads all my life, so I know where all the twists and turns are. We're going to take some side roads to bypass Dallas, but these are all roads that are used by neighboring ranchers, so they're easy enough to travel by buggy. Now, don't get me wrong. They all have rough places, so it's going to be a long and wearisome night. But as I said, we'll stop after a few hours and spend the night."

That didn't do much to make Candice relax as she listened to a group of coyotes yipping in the distance. She'd never spent the night outside, much less in the dark countryside in the mid-1800s.

She tried to remember any stories Grandma had told her of coyotes eating anyone, but couldn't remember anything like that. So maybe they'd be safe. Plus, she had Lucas to protect her, she thought, snuggling as close to him as she could get.

"Those coyotes sound kind of lonesome and spooky at the same time," Candice said, needing reassurance. "Do they eat people?"

"No. They mostly eat small animals. Sometimes they'll try to take down a cow or a horse, but normally they avoid humans," Lucas said reassuringly.

"What do you mean, 'normally'?" Candice asked, not feeling a lot better.

She heard the deep chuckle rumble in his chest. "It's going to be okay," he said. "I have my rifle, my handgun, and a double-barrel shotgun, so I can take care of any animal that tries to harm us. Two-legged or four-legged."

They rode in silence for a while. Candice kept thinking that now would be a good time to tell Lucas who she was and where she was from, but every time she opened her mouth to start the conversation, she backed out. Chickened out, was more like it, she chided herself. She knew she had to confess before they got married, but she decided she'd rather do it in the light so she could look into his eyes and watch his expression.

Mama Tanner's advice that talking to Lucas in the dark would be easier came back to Candice, and again, she wondered what Mama Tanner was talking about. Or why Mama Tanner would think Candice had anything to tell Lucas that would be easier to tell in the dark.

"Haw," Lucas said, breaking the silence and letting the horse know they were turning left. Candice had learned that "haw" in horse language meant to turn left, and "gee" meant to turn right.

"This road is a little smaller and a little rougher than the one we were on," Lucas said. "So you might want to hang onto my arm in case we hit a hole and bounce a little." He placed the arm that had been around her shoulder down beside him.

Candice wrapped both of her arms around Lucas's muscled one and lay her head on his shoulder. She was aware that this position pressed her breasts firmly against his arm, but she didn't care. They were going to be man and wife soon, so he might as well get to know a little about her body.

"Hmm. I like that," he said, kissing the top of her head.

Feeling content to just be here with him, Candice could feel herself start to relax. She had faith that he could take care of her if the need arose. She could feel herself begin to drift into sleep. She tried to fight it, but lost the battle.

Lucas could feel her relaxing as her handhold on his arm started to loosen. He wrapped his arm around her again to make sure she wouldn't bounce out of the buggy if he hit a bad rough spot.

He didn't know what the future held for them, and that made him a little nervous. Because he wanted to take care of her. He wanted to offer her a good life. He'd never been in love before, and he was amazed at the gentle feelings that flooded him every time he thought of her. Was he putting her life in danger by allowing her to become involved with him? Would their future be fraught with unrest and insecurities as he tried to find work and a place to live? Because the one thing he was sure of was that WW would take his ranch.

The ranch that his grandfather had tried so hard to turn into a paying ranch. Some things just didn't seem to be supposed to happen.

But the one thing that Lucas knew for sure was that wherever he was and whatever he was doing, he wanted this woman by his side.

ONCE LUCAS KNEW they were past Dallas and well on their way to Fort Worth, he contemplated where he'd want to stop for the night. He knew of several spots that'd be hidden from the road, yet those spots would be too open if someone accidentally came up on them in their sleep.

He remembered a barn that had been abandoned for several years. He wasn't sure whose land it was on, but if it still stood unused, he'd just stop there and let them rest for a few hours. He hated to disturb Candice since she slept so soundly, but he was beginning to be pretty weary and the horse could use a rest, so he'd go until he found the barn, then stop if he could see it in the dark. It stood a good way off the road.

Where was a good thunder storm when you needed some lightning to show you the way, he wondered. Then, as if he'd conjured it up, he saw distant lightning on the western horizon.

As Lucas watched the display he realized the storm was moving fairly quickly, and hoped he could find the barn before it hit. He'd hoped they could make their trip without a storm, but that wasn't going to happen.

He thought they were getting close to where the old barn stood, and was trying to make his eyes see through the dark. He was feeling frustrated when he made out the dim outline of a building and knew it was what he was looking for.

"Gee," he said to the horse, then loosened the reins in his hands to give the horse the freedom to find its way through this unfamiliar territory.

Apparently the horse could smell old hay in the barn, or other animals, because it headed straight toward the building. As they approached, the storm was getting closer. A flash of lightning lit up the sky and barn, letting Lucas see he'd been right about turning here.

The barn stood huge and noble against the dark. It had an opening in the middle, with stalls on each side. One stall had been closed in and had a door on it. A perfect place to take shelter from the weather and the night, if it wasn't full of unwanted guests. Like mice and other small animals.

Overhead, in the loft, Lucas could make out some scattered hay, and was happy the horse would have some food.

He guided the buggy into the opening, then pulled back on the reins to stop the horse. "I think this is going to be perfect, boy. We'll just take a break right here."

Candice came slowly awake at the sound of Lucas's voice and the motion of the stopping buggy. "Did I go to sleep?" she asked, looking groggily around. "Where are we?"

"Yes, you fell asleep. I guess you really do trust me to take care of you," Lucas said. "We're going to take shelter in this old barn for the rest of the night. And just in time, too, since there seems to be a major storm brewing."

As if to prove him right, a sharp flash of lightning struck ground not far from them, and a clap of thunder followed closely.

Then the rain hit, making a deafening noise on the old metal roof. The loud downpour startled the horse, and Lucas quickly unhitched him from the buggy and led him into one of the stalls and calmed him down. He left the bridle on the horse and loosely tied it to a post, so the horse could be free to nibble on old hay that still littered the floor.

Candice sat huddled in the buggy, looking around at the barn. This was a perfect place to spend the night, she decided. It sure beat sleeping on the ground, which she had no desire to experience.

Her heartbeat leaped as Lucas came out of the stall and headed toward her. This man would soon be her husband. She would spend the night with him tonight, but she knew he was too honorable to try and take advantage of her before they got married. How things had changed in the short time that had passed from this time period to the twenty-first century.

"Let me check this crib and see if it's decent for us to sleep in tonight," Lucas said, as he indicated the closed-in room on the other side of the buggy.

In a short while he came back, shaking his head. "No, I don't think we want to sleep in there," he said. "I heard too many scurrying feet when I opened the door. That's an old corn crib, and I think it's infested with mice and rats. And maybe a raccoon or two.

"See that ladder leading up into the hay loft? I'll go and see what it looks like up there. It'll probably be safer if we climb up there and sleep."

Watching Lucas go up the ladder while chills ran up and down her body just thinking about what was inside the crib, Candice was determined that she'd just sit here in the buggy and wait until daylight.

The storm still raged and didn't seem to be letting up. In fact, the wind seemed to be getting stronger. But maybe that was because the buggy sat in the hallway of the barn, and there might be a draft.

It seemed to be taking Lucas longer to check out the hayloft than it had taken him to check out the crib. Did that mean he wanted to sleep up there? Well, he could if he wanted to, but she was going to just sit right here.

Before long, she saw him coming down the ladder.

"Okay, there are a good many old bales of hay up there, and they don't seem to be infested with any varmints," Lucas declared. "So I've stacked some around and created a place to lie down and get some sleep."

"Well, I've decided that you can sleep up there if you want to, but I'm going to sit right here and wait until morning," Candice informed him.

She expected anything except the loud guffaw that escaped his mouth.

"Now, come on. You've trusted me to take care of you through the dark night, so can't you trust me to take care of you now?" His voice was amused, yet pleading, as he reached up and started to pull her toward him.

"Lucas! I don't want to go up there," Candice said, drawing back from him.

"But you'll be safer up there. This storm will play itself out eventually, then who knows what might come prowling around here."

"What do you mean? Wild animals? Coyotes? What?"

"Well, I don't think this barn is being used, but if it is, I don't know who owns it. So I'd rather be up there in the loft if somebody came to see what we're doing here.

"You sit here while I take the food and my guns up there, then I'll come back and help you get up the ladder, okay?"

"Okay. I guess. But it seems like being up there will kind of have us trapped if someone does come along."

"But it'll be like playing 'King of the Mountain.' They can't get up the ladder if we keep them pushed off. In fact, I'll pull the ladder up with us, and nobody can get up unless we let them."

"But neither can we get down," she reasoned.

"Then we'll have to come up with another plan if that happens. But I don't think it will," Lucas said, and began to unload the wagon.

Candice sat and watched him while the storm continued. Actually, she decided, this could be a wonderful romantic experience. Except for one small problem—

Chapter 19

"Lucas, I'm afraid of heights," Candice said as she stood in front of the ladder and saw how far up the loft was.

Lucas, who was standing directly behind her, moved close enough that the front part of his body was pressed against her back, then lifted his hands to the rung of the ladder and covered her hands. "Okay, here's what we'll do. You just put your foot on that first rung of the ladder and pull yourself up. As you pull up, I'll pull up with you. I won't let you fall. Don't look down. Just pull yourself up, one rung at a time. Okay?"

Just feeling his body pressed against her back was enough to take her mind off her fears. Almost. But she nodded her head and stepped up one rung. Lucas moved in unison with her, his body as if it were a part of her. As she bent her knee to step up, he bent his knee and put his foot on the rung hers had just left.

She could feel his warm breath on the back of her neck and cheek, and was getting warmer by the minute while chills ran up and down her body. She'd never been this affected by a man. Never!

She felt completely cocooned by him. His long arms had no trouble reaching up and around her to take hold of the next highest rung on the ladder, while his larger shoulders and body pressed against hers and pushed her upward. They both were breathing hard, and they both knew it wasn't because of the exertion from climbing the ladder.

Before she knew it, Candice had pulled herself up high enough that she could see into the loft. She'd been so aware of Lucas and what they were experiencing that she hadn't realized how high she'd come.

"Okay, this is where you'll really have to trust me. Just climb up until you can get your foot on the floor of the loft, then pull yourself on in. Hold on to the sides of the ladder when you get to the top rung, then just push or pull yourself into the loft," Lucas directed from behind. His voice was odd sounding, and Candice was glad he couldn't see the smile she had to fight. *If Grandma could see me now,* she thought.

Very hesitantly she pulled herself high enough that she could put one foot on the floor. Using the two pieces of the ladder that extended above the top rung, she pushed herself into the loft. She was sorry when she lost contact with Lucas's body, but happy that she was on something solid again.

Lucas came in behind her and took her hand. When lightning flashed, he pointed to a spot in the back of the barn. "I made us a place to sleep back there," he said. He began to lead her in that direction.

With the continual flashing of the lightning, Candice could see that he had placed bales of hay in a square, with enough of an opening for them to walk into their "sleeping quarters."

"I cut a bale of hay open and spread it out, then spread this old quilt that I brought with us over the hay. This will be a lot better than sleeping on the ground," he said.

"I agree," Candice said. "I'm glad you forced me to climb up here."

"I'm glad, too," Lucas said. And he was glad that he'd managed to keep her from becoming aware of how much their position had been affecting him.

"Do you want to eat something before we lie down?" he asked.

"No. I'm not hungry, but you eat if you are."

"I'm not hungry either," he said. Not for food, at least, he thought. How was he going to make it through this night? It had been a big enough problem at times just knowing she was just down the hall when they were at home. But now they would be close together. Alone. On a stormy night, with rain pounding on the metal roof.

Lucas hadn't realized that he'd groaned out loud until Candice asked, "Lucas, are you okay?"

"I'm fine," he lied. He sat down on the quilt and held his hand up to hers. "Come on and let's get settled in and try to get some rest," he said.

She sat beside him and looked around at the walls of hay surrounding them. The sweet smell of old hay filled her senses, but she was looking to see if there were any straggling varmints in the hay bales.

Lucas immediately realized what she was doing, and chuckled. "I made pretty sure there were no lingering pests in these bales I stacked around us. I bounced them around on the floor for a few times to scare any mice or snakes out."

Candice could hear the teasing in his voice, but that didn't make her feel any better at all.

Seeing her eyes flash in the lightning, Lucas laughed and pulled her down with him as he lay back on the quilt. "We'll be fine. Any creatures in this barn are more afraid of us than we are of them. Come on and let's try to get some sleep."

Candice turned on her side, away from Lucas. He turned with her, and although they weren't touching, like they had been on the ladder, his body was close enough that she could feel his heat.

She had to get her mind off of this man so she could go to

sleep. She hadn't had any problem holding onto his arm and sleeping in the buggy, but this was entirely different.

"Candice? You're safe with me. I respect you too much to try and take advantage of you in a situation like this."

"I know," Candice answered, wishing he'd at least kiss her goodnight. But that was probably not a good thing to do, under the circumstances.

She tried to calm down and keep her mind on the rain that had quieted down to a gentle pattering on the old metal roof of the barn. The thunder was now distant and drifting away. Without being aware of it, she eased into a deep sleep.

Lucas, on the other hand, couldn't keep his mind off of the woman who lay gently breathing so close to him that all he had to do was reach out and wrap his arm around her waist and pull her against him.

He tried listening to the slowly departing storm. He tried thinking about what would happen when they got back to the ranch and Willard Williams discovered that he was married. He tried to think about where he and Candice would live and where he would work when WW took the ranch. And finally, his tired brain gave up and he drifted into a restless sleep.

CANDICE CAME SLOWLY awake, realizing that sunlight was shining on her face. She gradually opened her eyes and looked right into the clear blue eyes of Lucas Tanner. For a moment she was disoriented and wondered what Lucas was doing in her bed. Then she remembered where they were.

"You are so beautiful," Lucas said. "Your hair looks like burnished gold in the sunlight. And your eyes are as green as the fresh grass on a cool spring morning. I want to wake up every day of my life and see you come awake beside me. I'm so happy you agreed to marry me. I can't wait to make you mine completely."

Before Candice could answer, a loud voice from below them

bellowed, "Hello, the loft! Anybody up there! Come where I can see you with your hands up!"

"You stay right here and let me handle this," Lucas said, reaching for the pistol that was on the floor beside him.

"I'm coming!" Lucas shouted. "Stay calm. I just needed a place to get out of the storm last night."

He stood and stuck the pistol in the back waistband of his jeans, then slowly moved forward so the person below could see him.

"Lucas Thornton?" the voice said as Lucas got within view of the man below.

"Jim Hawthorne!" Lucas broke into a laugh. "Is this your barn?" he asked, going down the ladder.

Candice could hear the voices below, but couldn't make out what they were saying. So she sat, hidden by the bales of hay, and waited for Lucas to come back. She sucked in a deep breath of relief that the person who had found them was someone who knew Lucas and sounded friendly enough.

It seemed like forever before the voices stopped and Lucas climbed back to her. She could immediately tell by his face that something was wrong.

"We've got to get out of here," he said, beginning to gather up their food basket and the other things he'd brought up for the night. "We'll have to grab a bite to eat as we ride, I guess.

"That was Jim Hawthorne, and this barn is on his ranch, but Willard Williams is on his way to talk with Jim about the ranch. Jim has decided, after much pressure from WW, to sell his ranch to him.

"Jim's wife died a couple of years ago, and they never had any children, so he's decided to head back to West Texas, where he grew up. But he knows what trouble WW is causing the ranchers around Dallas, so he suggested I get away before Willard shows up."

They hurriedly got everything back into the buggy and the

horse back in the harness. Two horsemen in the distance were galloping toward them as they headed down the lane from the barn to the main road.

"That was a close call," Lucas said as he guided the horse and buggy back onto the road and headed toward Fort Worth.

A chill crept up Candice's spine, just thinking about what might have happened if Willard Williams had found them in the barn.

But Willard Williams was going to find out about them eventually. Even though they got away this time, the time would come when they'd have to face the cold-blooded WW.

The chill stayed with Candice for a while.

Taking a deep breath, Candice knew it was time for her to confess her secret to Lucas. Apprehension clogged her throat as she wondered how he'd take the news.

Did she really have to tell him? She'd made up her mind that she wanted to stay with him, here in his time period, so why did he need to know? Wouldn't she be taking a chance of destroying what they had?

Or what she thought they had, that small, irritating voice reminded her. How would he react if he knew the truth about her?

But he never has to know, she argued with the voice in her head.

It's just not right to go into a marriage with this kind of secret between you, the voice persisted.

"Oh, all right," she said loudly.

Lucas jumped at her voice, and the horse's ears perked up and twitched.

"Are you okay?" Lucas asked.

Candice hid the giggle that had almost escaped her at the reaction of Lucas and the horse. She really hadn't meant to say that out loud.

"Lucas, I've got something I really need to talk with you

about. I shouldn't have waited this long, but I was afraid if I told you it would change the way you feel about me."

"There's nothing you could tell me that would change my feelings for you, Candice. I never thought I'd find anyone to love. I thought I'd be damned to living a loveless life with Mary Beth, then you came along and changed everything. Somehow your just being here has made it possible for me to escape Willard Williams and Mary Beth.

"Besides, we're almost to Fort Worth, so we need to be discussing our wedding, don't you think?"

It was almost as if Lucas was afraid to let her tell him what was on her mind. Was he afraid it really would change his mind about her?

"But if you want to tell me, go ahead. As far as I can guess, we're about thirty minutes from Fort Worth."

Candice knew she couldn't explain to him all he'd want to know about her previous life in thirty minutes, so she said, "No, that's okay. It really isn't that important, anyway."

Not that important? You're from another time period where things are totally different from what it is here and it's not that important?

"I'm really sorry about the rush of our wedding. I know most women like their wedding to be special, with a lot of family and friends around. Maybe once we get home and get settled somewhere, we can have another ceremony with all those things for you," Lucas said.

"Lucas, I'm not like most women when it comes to things like that. In my opinion, being married is the same whether there's a big deal made or not."

"You're a special kind of woman, Candice. I hope you know that," Lucas said.

You have no idea how special I am, Candice thought, but said, "Thank you. I hope you never change your mind about that."

Chapter 20

THEY REACHED FORT WORTH MIDMORNING, TO THE HUS-
tle and bustle of people everywhere. Horses and buggies,
horses with riders, and people hurrying or strolling through
the streets, just like they'd done in Dallas. Not as many people
as there had been in Dallas—still, more than Candice had expected.

Lucas seemed to know exactly where he was going as he
turned the horse and buggy down a side street and kept going
until a small wooden church appeared ahead of them. A mod-
est house was to the right of the church. Candice guessed this
was the parsonage, as Lucas stopped the horse in front of the
house.

Almost immediately, a short, plump woman came to the
door.

"Hello, Mrs. Duncan," Lucas said, getting out of the buggy.
"Is Preacher Duncan at home?"

"Yes, he's in the church, preparing his sermon for Sunday,"
she answered.

"I hate to interrupt him, but my fiancée and I need to talk
with him about getting married as soon as possible." As he
talked, Lucas came around to Candice's side of the buggy and

lifted his arms to help her down.

"Is that you, Lucas Thornton?" the woman asked, coming closer.

"Yes, ma'am," Lucas said, leading Candice toward the woman. "And this is my fiancée, Candice Moore. Candice, this is Mrs. Annabelle Duncan. She and Preacher Duncan used to live in Dallas until they decided to move here and try and save all the sinners in Fort Worth."

Mrs. Duncan gave a hearty laugh. "Lucas, you haven't changed a bit. How's Mama Tanner?" She wrapped Lucas in a warm hug.

"She's just as bossy as she ever was," Lucas answered. "She said to give you her best wishes, if we saw you. She misses the times you and her spent together."

"I miss her, too. I haven't found such a good friend here in Fort Worth. Good friends are hard to come by."

Just then a huge man who looked like he'd just stepped off a horse stuck his head out of the church door. "What's all the commotion out here? Is that Lucas Thornton's voice I hear?"

"You might as well come on out here and see for yourself," Lucas said, heading toward the man. "You can't hide in God's house all day and try to escape the world."

Instead of shaking hands, the two men grabbed each other in a big bear hug.

"We love that boy like he's our own," Mrs. Duncan said. "George took him under his wings when Lucas's parents disappeared. He figured Lucas needed a male figure in his life." She took Candice's hand and headed back up the steps to the front door. "Come on inside and let me get you a glass of tea."

Lucas and the preacher were busy talking, so Candice allowed the woman to lead her into the small but lovely house.

Homey. That was the first word that came to Candice's mind as she glanced around the living room. She only had time to come up with a brief impression, though, as Mrs.

Duncan was leading her quickly into a kitchen and dining room combination. "Just sit down here at the table and I'll get us some iced tea," the woman said. "The ice man just delivered a fresh block of ice this morning."

There was an ice box at the ranch, but Candice had never been aware that there'd been any ice in it. She'd wondered about it at times, but never asked. The ice would probably have melted by the time they got home from Dallas with it, she'd speculated.

"Here you go," Mrs. Duncan said, setting a large glass in front of Candice, who immediately picked it up and took a big sip.

She almost got tears in her eyes because the tea was so good and she hadn't seen ice or had iced tea since she'd arrived in this time period. "This is wonderful!" she said, after she'd gotten her emotions under control.

"Thank you. George loves his iced tea. Now, tell me about you. Where are you from? You didn't grow up around Dallas, did you? I don't remember ever hearing about any Moores in the area."

Wow. Not what Candice had expected to run into. Why hadn't Lucas told her about the Duncans so she could be prepared with her story? Of course, Lucas didn't know she needed to prepare a story for anyone.

Her mind was in a tail spin. She didn't want to out-and-out lie to a preacher's wife. Actually, she didn't want to lie to anyone, and she hadn't been forced to lie to the Thorntons, since they'd just taken Gramma's thoughts about her being "one of the New York Johnstons" and gone with it.

"My grandmother and a lot of my Johnston relatives are buried at the cemetery close to Lucas's ranch. My dad was a Moore, but my mom and dad were killed in an accident when I was very young. My grandmother raised me. Some of our relatives live in New York." *At least that's what Gramma*

Thornton said, Candice added mentally.

"Oh, so you're from the old Johnston family. You know that Lucas's grandparents bought that ranch and house from a Johnston, don't you?"

"Yes, I do know that," Candice said, hoping the subject could be changed. Relief flooded her when she heard Lucas and Preacher Duncan coming in the back door.

"Mama, these two youngsters will be spending the night with us tonight. They want me to marry them, and they've just gotten into town and need a place to stay."

"But we couldn't impose on you like that!" Candice said.

"That's what I told him," Lucas said. "But he insisted."

"Well, of course you'll stay with us. We have two spare bedrooms, so it won't be a problem at all. This house is too empty since our Jimmy and Alice got married and moved into houses of their own."

"But—"

"There's really no arguing with this man, Candice," Lucas told her. "I've known him most of my life and he may be a preacher, but he's the most bull-headed person I've ever met. He's even worse than Mama Tanner, once he gets dug in."

"And I know that even better than you do, Lucas," Mrs. Duncan said.

Everyone laughed, but Candice didn't feel comfortable staying here under Mrs. Duncan's watchful eyes. She almost felt as if the woman knew her secret. Or at least that Candice had a secret of some kind.

Seemingly caught in the trap, Candice helped Mrs. Duncan put fresh sheets on the beds that had once been her children's. The furniture in the Duncans' son's room was sparse, because guys didn't have need for much furniture in that time period. And it was sturdy, as if to take the roughness of a boy. Candice noticed several marks on the bedstead that looked like someone had tried to carve the wood. She couldn't help but smile, thinking of a little boy in overalls with bare feet, trying to carve his name on the bedstead.

The furniture in the daughter's room was more ornate, with a rose pattern on the bedstead and chest of drawers.

Mrs. Duncan talked about the children the entire time they were getting the beds ready for the night. After they'd finished, she stood straight and stretched her back. "I miss my babies so much, but I have to say my workload is a lot easier now that they're not here.

"Don't get me wrong. I loved them as much as a mother can, and they had their chores. Still—well, you'll understand when you and Lucas start having babies. It's not an easy life here, I can tell you that much."

Before Candice could figure out how to ask what she meant by her last statement, Mrs. Duncan continued. "Okay, we may as well go and get some food ready for the men. You can never keep a man full for very long."

She headed straight for the pie safe and took out a plate with sliced cornbread on it and handed it to Candice. "Set that on the table, if you will."

Then she proceeded to take out several bowls that obviously contained leftovers from the noon meal. There was a bowl of baby lima beans, corn, fried okra, fresh sliced tomatoes and cucumbers, and an apple pie.

Noticing that the bowls were still warm, Candice asked, "Did you cook all of this food this morning?"

"Yes. I like to get my days' worth of cooking done before the heat sets in. So I cook breakfast and dinner at the same time. Then at supper, we just eat leftovers."

Candice knew that that was done especially in the summertime, but Mama Tanner usually cooked three meals a day because of having to feed the cowboys.

They had barely finished setting the food on the table before the men came in. "See what I told you?" Mrs. Duncan said to

Candice. "They can smell the food even if they're a mile away from the house."

"Oh, woman! Stop your nagging," Mr. Duncan said. "You know my stomach knows when it's time to eat. You make me eat breakfast before sunup every day just so you can get your cooking done." Mr. Duncan proceeded to give his wife a big kiss, right in front of Candice and Lucas.

Mrs. Duncan giggled like a schoolgirl and slapped him on the shoulder. "You and Lucas go wash your hands before this food gets any colder than it is. You'll be the one nagging tonight when you eat it and it's cold."

Candice watched in amazement as the older couple actually flirted with each other. Would she and Lucas still be flirting like that when they were that age?

It occurred to her that this was the first time she'd thought of her and Lucas growing old together.

That is, if he still wanted to marry her if she told him her secret.

Chapter 21

As they ate the wonderful meal Mrs. Duncan had prepared and everyone told her how much they enjoyed the food, it dawned on Candice that Lucas was used to eating food that had been prepared by really good cooks.

She felt a jolt of nerves as she realized that not only were Mama Tanner and Mrs. Duncan great cooks, they knew how to cook the food Lucas was used to. Candice was learning by helping Mama Tanner, but now that she and Lucas would be married, she wouldn't have Mama Tanner around to help her. *Just another reason this marriage shouldn't take place,* her rational brain whispered.

"Candice, are you okay?" Lucas's concerned voice asked.

"Yes, I'm fine," she lied. "I'm just lost in all the tastes of this food. Lucas, you need to be forewarned that I can't cook anything like Mrs. Duncan or Mama Tanner."

"I'll be content with whatever you come up with," he said, looking deeply into her eyes.

"Now, that's true love," Mr. Duncan said. "And it's good to see Lucas in love with a good woman. I was really worried about him during this Willard Williams situation."

"But you don't have anything to worry about now, do you?"

Mrs. Duncan asked Lucas.

"Well, I fully expect WW to take my ranch as soon as he learns about my marriage to Candice. In fact, he'd already threatened to take it as soon as Gramma died, so now that she's gone I expect him to make his move any moment. I'm sure he'll make the move as soon as he hears about the wedding."

"Isn't there anything you can do to keep him from taking your place?" Mr. Duncan asked.

"No. My grandfather was already too far in debt to the bank when he died. WW agreed to let the standing agreement continue when he took over the bank. But he made it clear he was only doing it out of respect for Gramma, and that he'd make his move as soon as she was gone."

"Harrumph," Mr. Duncan said. "That man never respected anyone. I'll bet my money he was using that agreement to hold over your head to get you to marry that daughter of his."

"I've suspected that," Lucas said.

"Well, know this, Lucas. If you find yourself without your ranch and a job, you and Candice are always welcome to come stay with us until you can find your own place."

"And you can even share one bed, if you stay here after you're married," Mrs. Duncan said.

"Mama! You're a wicked woman for having such thoughts," Mr. Duncan chided, but couldn't hide the twinkle in his eyes.

"I thank you for that, George," Lucas said. "But I couldn't take advantage of your hospitality."

"Hush your mouth, Lucas Thornton," Mrs. Duncan exclaimed. "You grew up playing with my children, in and out of our house, when we lived close to you. You're just like one of my own, and I couldn't turn you away any more than I could my own kids. Now, I don't want to hear any more about it, you hear me?"

"Yes ma'am," Lucas said. As soon as she stood up to start cleaning the food off the table, he stood and wrapped her in a warm hug. Then he proceeded to do the same thing to Mr. Duncan.

"You all will never know how much you helped me after my parents disappeared. You made me feel like I still had a family. Now, don't get me wrong. Mama Tanner and Gramma took extremely good care of me, but your home helped me remember what a home with both parents should feel like."

"You were always a pleasure to have around, son," Mr. Duncan said.

Candice could tell he was fighting his emotions. They really loved Lucas. It showed in their faces, eyes and voices. She only remembered feeling that kind of love from Grandma.

And now, from Lucas. She felt loved every time he looked at her.

"Lucas, why don't you and Candice go sit in the living room and relax. I know it was a hard trip from Dallas for you. I'll take care of this food and these few dishes, then I'll join you," Mrs. Duncan said.

"I'll go finish up the paperwork I was doing in the church, and I'll join you, too," Mr. Duncan added.

"But—" Candice was about to argue about helping with the kitchen.

"Go on and rest, child. I can see that you're so tired you're about to doze off at the table."

Embarrassed that she must look that bad, Candice said, "It was kind of a long trip for me."

Obediently, Lucas and Candice went into the living room. Lucas sat in a rocking chair at the end of the couch, and Candice sat on the end of the couch closest to him.

They'd barely gotten comfortable when Candice said in a hushed voice, "Why didn't you tell me we were coming here?"

"I wasn't sure they'd even still be here. Their daughter lives in Oklahoma and has been urging them to move close to her. So I thought they may have already moved. It's been a while since I've seen them.

"But it's okay if you didn't know we were coming, isn't it? I didn't think it mattered one way or the other."

"It's just that I wasn't prepared to meet some of your friends," Candice said.

Chuckling, Lucas asked, "So what did you need to do to get prepared? It's not like we could have stopped on the side of the road and let you take a bath or anything."

"I'm talking about getting mentally prepared. There's just something about getting mentally prepared for something like this that makes me feel more relaxed." She could tell Lucas wasn't taking her seriously at all. In fact, he seemed to be trying to hide a smile. Suddenly she realized how silly she sounded, and started to giggle.

That's all it took for Lucas to start laughing. The more they laughed, the funnier it got.

It felt good to be laughing with Lucas. It felt right. Somehow Candice felt more connected with him, now, than she had before.

"Are you two okay?" Mrs. Duncan asked from the kitchen doorway.

"Yes, ma'am," Lucas said, wiping the tears from his eyes. "We're a lot better now that we've gotten rid of a little tension."

"Okay. But I really like the sound of you laughing together. Being able to laugh together helps to build a strong marriage," she said, and went back to the kitchen.

"Speaking of marriage," Lucas said, "If it's okay with you, we'll just go in the morning to get our marriage license, then George can marry us tomorrow afternoon. Maybe we can spend the night in a hotel tomorrow night, then head back to the ranch the next day. Does that sound okay?"

Reality hit Candice hard. She was actually about to get married to a man who had been born a hundred and forty one years before she was. A man who had only known what life was like in the 1800s. A man who had no idea where she was from or anything about her. What was she about to do?

She could feel her heart rate accelerating to a feverish point. Her hands were beginning to sweat. Her vision seemed blurry as she looked at Lucas.

Instantly, he realized that something was wrong and slid out of the rocking chair to kneel in front of her. Taking both of her hands in his, he said, "Candice? Are you okay? Please don't tell me you're getting cold feet. I love you so much. Please don't back out of the wedding. I don't know how I'd go on without you. You've become my life. You're all that I think of."

Looking at this large, rugged rancher kneeling in front of her brought Candice out of her temporary panic attack. Taking her hands from his and placing them on each side of his face, she gently put her lips on his for a moment.

"Of course your plans for tomorrow are okay with me, Lucas. Whatever you think is best. I do love you, and I want to spend my life with you. It's just that it hit me that this was actually about to happen. You and I are actually going to get married! And it was just overwhelming for a moment."

He leaned over and captured her lips in a kiss that was at once calming and exciting. He would have kept deepening the kiss if they hadn't heard a sound in the room with them. They looked up to find the Duncans standing in the doorway with huge smiles on their faces.

"Maybe all I need to do is pronounce you man and wife, at this point," Mr. Duncan teased with a chuckle.

Lucas got quickly to his feet and sat back down in the rocking chair, looking like a child who had gotten caught with his hand in the cookie jar.

"George, don't embarrass the boy," Mrs. Duncan said.

"Oh, don't worry about that, Mama. The boy has already taken care of that on his own."

"I'm sorry to be carrying on like that in your home," Lucas

apologized.

"Nonsense," Mrs. Duncan said. "You're just showing normal, healthy affection for the woman you love. Don't ever apologize for that, and don't ever stop doing it. A married couple needs to continue being affectionate as long as they live. That keeps the love strong. Even when you get to the age that sex isn't as important as it is when you're young, you still need to show each other affection," Mrs. Duncan said, very strongly.

Shocked at her open declaration of how a husband and wife should act, Candice could only sit and look at her hands.

But Mr. Duncan burst out laughing. "Lucas, you remember who taught you boys about the birds and bees, don't you? It was Mama, here, not me. I was too busy and kept putting it off until I had time. But the truth is, I never felt comfortable talking about all that stuff, and I figured that since you grew up around animals, you probably knew all you needed to know, so Mama stepped in and took care of it."

"That's because all animals do is have sex in order to have babies. Those boys needed to know that there's more to a marriage than just having sex. A woman needs to know she's loved. She needs to be handled gently. Especially when it comes to the bedroom. I didn't want my boys to approach their wives like a bull ready to mate."

"Well, now, Mama, some things just come normal. I never had anyone tell me what to do, and I don't really believe that I approached you like a mating bull. Did I?" Suddenly Mr. Duncan didn't sound so sure of himself.

"No, love, you're a very wonderful, gentle lover. I could never have imagined anyone better than you. But everyone doesn't have those natural loving instincts."

Too much information! Too much information! Candice thought, feeling her face turn beet red.

"Now, Mama, you've embarrassed both of them," Mr. Duncan teasingly scolded his wife. "I'll tell you what. This woman has been this way ever since I met her fifty-one years ago. She's always talked and acted as if there was no reason to keep a watch over her tongue. She says what others are thinking but don't have the guts to say. I've always been intrigued by her attitude, but sometimes, as a minister's wife, she may go just a little overboard."

"Overboard? A minister's wife? George Duncan, if a minister and his wife can't tell a young couple how married life is supposed to be, then who else is going to counsel them?" Indignation sounded in every word that came out of Mrs. Duncan's mouth.

"See what I mean? Just like that word 'counsel.' Nobody else uses words like that around here. She uses words you'd expect some uppity judge or someone from England to use. She's just amazing." He gazed at his wife with love and affection.

"Lucas, why don't you and me go outside and I'll show you the fine garden I've got going this summer," Mr. Duncan said. "Summer's almost over and so is the garden, but you can see what was in it."

As soon as the men went out the back door, Mrs. Duncan turned to Candice and asked, "Have you told him yet?"

"Told him what?" Candice was afraid to ask.

"That you're a Traveler."

Chapter 22

"H—how did you know?" Candice asked. This was the second time she'd been asked that since she'd arrived in this time. First Dr. Wilson, now Mrs. Duncan.

"You have the look that's easy to recognize if you're not from here yourself. Just like you would know something was off if Lucas or George came to your time period. You would know."

Thinking about it, Candice realized Mrs. Duncan was right. "So are you a Traveler?" she asked Mrs. Duncan.

"Yes. I came here in 1970. I came through the cemetery, like I'm assuming you did." When Candice nodded in agreement, Mrs. Duncan continued. "I'd just buried my first husband, Tom, my only living relative, and I was having a horrible time of it. I'd go to the cemetery every day and sit by his grave and mourn for him. We'd only been married for five years and were just planning to start a family. He was in construction and a steel beam fell on him and killed him instantly.

"When I stumbled out of the cemetery I wasn't far from the road. George was passing by on his horse and spotted me. He took me to a friend's house in Dallas, and she let me stay with her while I got a job in one of the department stores. She became my best friend.

"George and I were friends for two years before we got married. Well, he wanted to be more than friends, but it took me that long to get over Tom. But I finally realized I could love again, so George and I got married."

She paused, as if remembering all of it, so Candice asked, "Does Mr. Duncan know?"

"No. I meant to tell him. But the longer I got to know George, the more I realized that I didn't think he'd handle my situation very well.

"After I'd been here for about a year, I met an older woman who was a Traveler, and she and I became friends. She came here when she was a young girl, but she still remembered how weird it was to be in a different place and time. So she helped me come to grips with it, some.

"But when George found out I was friends with her, he got really upset and told me I shouldn't hang around with her. Of course I asked why, and he said she wasn't from around here and that folks thought she was crazy.

"I didn't stop being her friend, and I'm so happy that I didn't because she died the next year, right before George and I got married.

"But I knew from his reaction that if I told him, he wouldn't want to be around me anymore. And by then I was realizing I had feelings for him and didn't want to lose him.

"I also knew that I didn't want to go back to where I'd come from. It was too sad for me there, even if I did know how to get back. I went to the cemetery several times trying to find the portal, but decided that I didn't want to find it because then I might be tempted to go back.

"So I didn't tell him. We got married, and I adjusted to life in this time very well. But mind you, we were in Dallas, and living there was a lot easier than living on the ranch where Lucas lives.

"Anyway, we have two beautiful children. Georgette, who is

thirty and living in Oklahoma with her husband, Hank, and their little girl, Amy, and she's pregnant with another child. And we have Aaron, who is twenty-eight and living in Houston. Neither of them know about me, either.

"Georgette wants George and me to move close to her. Hank has a large family and they all live around there, so I'm sure she'll stay in that area. George and I are planning on moving there to be close to the grandchildren. But tell me how you wound up here."

Candice told her the entire story, and had Mrs. Duncan laughing out loud at some of the antics from Lucas's grandmother and Mama Tanner. She was especially amused at the story about Diablo.

Candice felt a connection with Mrs. Duncan, and was immediately sad because the Duncans were moving away. Mrs. Duncan would make a wonderful friend. Someone that Candice could go to if and when she became discouraged about living in this time. Someone who would understand where she was coming from.

"Wow! I think you've had a much harder time settling in than I did. I'm thankful I didn't have to go through all that," Mrs. Duncan said, interrupting Candice's thoughts. "But you know that it's strictly your business whether you tell Lucas or not."

Apparently Mrs. Duncan didn't know about Dr. Wilson being a Traveler, because she didn't mention him.

"Who delivered your children?" Candice asked. Surely Dr. Wilson would have recognized Mrs. Duncan as a Traveler, like he did her.

"We had a neighbor who delivered babies, so we just used her. She was really good, and my babies came easily, so I didn't need a doctor. Why do you ask?"

"Did you ever go to Dr. Wilson for anything?" Candice asked, trying not alert any suspicion.

Smiling, Mrs. Duncan said, "Yes, George and I used him for ourselves and for our children when we needed him. He's a nice man. I always wondered about him being a Traveler, but was afraid to ask. He just seemed to know a lot about medicine for the time. Is he a Traveler?"

Wishing she hadn't said anything, Candice said, "Yes. But promise me you won't mention it to anyone. Especially that I told you. I don't want him to think I'm telling his story."

"Oh, don't you worry about that. George and I will be long gone from Dallas in a few months, so I won't even be in the area. So did he recognize you or did you recognize him?"

"He treated my scratch after Diablo attacked me, and asked if I was a Traveler. He said something about my clothes and scent reminding him of the wife he'd lost in a car accident. I was so shocked to find someone who knew how I felt. And now I've found you, but you'll be moving away.

"But I did find the portal back. I don't know if you want to know that or not, but I found it between two of my third-great aunts' graves."

"So, if you're marrying Lucas, I guess you've decided to stay here, even though you could go back if you want to."

"Yes, I've decided to stay. And I've about decided to not tell Lucas. It just seems like that would be less confusing to him. Especially now that I've talked with you. You've made it work out, so I'm sure I can."

"How did you find the portal?"

"I was in the cemetery, and I'd just had a big argument with Willard Williams. He'd left and a sudden thunderstorm came up. A bolt of lightning struck very close to me, and suddenly I could see the portal between the graves and I got a brief glimpse of Grandma's grave in the future time. As you know, that grave isn't in the cemetery in this time.

"But when we were there for Lucas's grandmother's burial I went back and checked, and as I got close to where I thought it was, the air in a certain spot looked hazy with a slight shimmering to it, so I knew it was really there."

"Do you think you'll ever try to go back?"

"I don't think so. Grandma was my only living relative that I'm aware of, and I didn't have many friends. So there's really nothing there for me to go back to. Other than," she added, chuckling, "a much easier way of life. But now that I have Lucas to love and have him love me in return, I don't even care about that."

"Do you ever wonder if other people who disappear have gone through the portal?" Mrs. Duncan asked.

"I did kind of think about that," Candice said.

"You know that Lucas's parents just disappeared one day. Nobody has ever heard a word from them, and I've always wondered if they'd gone through and couldn't find their way back.

"I know that was one sad little boy for a long time after his parents left. But his mother never did seem like a happy woman. She always seemed out of place somehow or other."

Chapter 23

MID-AFTERNOON OF THE NEXT DAY, LUCAS AND CANDICE stood in the church in front of Mr. Duncan as he prepared to start the marriage ceremony. He'd put on a clergy's robe that instantly changed him from the friend, Mr. Duncan, to the minister.

Candice could feel her heart rate accelerate and her palms getting sweaty. She was actually about to marry Lucas Thornton. She was actually planning to stay in this time, when everything was so much harder, in ways, than what she was used to. And yet life was so much simpler, quieter, and more relaxed than the future Dallas and what she was used to.

The Duncans had asked a friend to stand with Lucas, and Mrs. Duncan stood with Candice, as witnesses to the wedding. They'd ask the church pianist to play a couple of songs before the wedding started.

Suddenly she had a longing for Grandma to know what was happening with her. *Oh, Grandma. How would you advise me on this? What would you do if this happened to you?*

Go with your heart. A small voice of reason came to Candice, and she knew that was exactly what Grandma had always told her. *Thank you, Grandma.*

"Candice? Candice, are you okay?" She became aware of Lucas's voice close to her ear.

"Yes, I'm fine," she said, looking up into the blue eyes of the man she loved. "I'm really happy," she said. And realized that she was.

"You may kiss the bride," Mr. Duncan said, with a big smile on his face.

Lucas drew Candice into his arms and covered her mouth with his. This kiss was different than the ones they'd shared before. Lucas poured his soul into the kiss, as if giving all of himself to her. She felt herself doing the same thing. This was a kiss of two people committing to a lifetime of love.

"Ahem! You may stop kissing the bride, now," Mr. Duncan said.

Reluctantly they pulled apart, and everyone started laughing as the newlyweds' faces turned red.

Just then the church door burst open and Johnny Lamb burst into the room, then came to a screeching halt when he realized what he was interrupting. "I'm sorry, boss. I'll just sit here and wait until you all are finished."

"It's okay, Johnny," Lucas said. "I've just married the love of my life. Come on down here and congratulate us, then tell us what's wrong."

"Congratulations," Johnny said, shaking Lucas's hand, then giving Candice a hug and a kiss on the cheek. "Sorry, boss, but I just had to do that since you snatched this beautiful woman away from the rest of us."

Candice felt her face turning red again at his unexpected compliment.

"But boss, something terrible has happened at the ranch. Someone shot Willard Williams and the sheriff's looking for you."

"Is WW dead?" Lucas asked.

"Yes. And he was killed on your ranch! Mama Tanner sent

me to get you. She said you might be here at the Duncans'. She said to tell you to get back as fast as you can after you're married, but wait until dark before you come to the house. She thinks the place is being watched. The sheriff's been asking her and others if they know where you are. She said to watch your back at all times, because she's afraid some of WW's hired hands will start looking for you and try to hang you as soon as they find you, instead of bringing you back to Dallas to stand trial.

"I rode as hard as I could to get here, and now I'm heading back so nobody will get suspicious that I'm gone."

"Well, before you leave, you have to come to the house and eat a good meal," Mrs. Duncan spoke up.

"That's right, Johnny," Lucas agreed. "I'm sure you haven't stopped to rest you or your horse since you left the ranch. I'll get your horse some food and water while you eat and rest a few minutes.

"In fact, I'll saddle the horse that I used to pull the buggy here, because your horse is probably pretty winded. My buggy horse might not be as fast as your horse, but she'll get you there."

"Well, I did push Charley a mite hard," Johnny said. "But he may not take kindly to pulling a buggy back to Dallas."

"He'll be fine. I'll take it nice and easy on him. I don't want anyone who may see us to think we're in a hurry to get any-where in particular, anyway," Lucas said.

AFTER JOHNNY HAD EATEN and rested for about an hour, he was ready to get back on the road toward Dallas.

"So what are your plans?" Mrs. Duncan asked Lucas as they watched Johnny ride away.

"My gut tells me to leave Candice here, until I can get to Dallas and find out what's going on," Lucas said, looking at Candice.

"No," Candice said.

"Now, Candice, why don't you just think about this for a moment?" Mrs. Duncan said. "That does make sense. Lucas could take the horse and travel a lot faster by himself. Also, if trouble did arise on the way there, you'd be safer here."

"No. I didn't marry Lucas to hide from any trouble that came our way. If there's going to be trouble, and it seems like there will be, I want to be there to help him."

"But, Candice—"

"Lucas Thornton! Don't try to change my mind on this. I'm going home with you," Candice declared. Then looking at the Duncans, she said, "I really appreciate your offer, but I need to be with my husband."

"You got yourself one strong woman, Lucas," Mr. Duncan spoke up. "And I agree with her. Two people in a buggy, riding along together like husband and wife, will be a lot less conspicuous than a man on a horse in a hurry to get somewhere."

"Thank you, Mr. Duncan," Candice said.

"I guess you're right, George, as much as I don't like the idea," Lucas said. Then looking at Candice with a twinkle in his eyes, "Is this the way our marriage is going to be? Are you going to argue with me every time I try to make a decision?"

"If you make decisions I agree with, I promise you there won't be an argument," Candice said, smiling sweetly.

"I can see this is going to be a long and happy marriage," Mrs. Duncan said, and laughed.

"I'm not sure when we should try to travel," Lucas said. "If we leave tonight, we won't be able to make it all the way there before sunrise, so we'll have to find a place to wait until it gets dark before going on in. But if we leave in the morning, we'll be taking a chance of being spotted more easily."

"I have a suggestion," Mr. Duncan said. "Wait and leave early in the morning. I have an old clergy's robe you can wear. And Mama, you give Candice one of your bonnets to wear.

That way you'll look like a minister with his wife, and nobody looking for Lucas Thornton will ever think of him as a minister."

"That's an excellent idea, George," Mrs. Duncan said. "Come on, Candice. Show me which dress you'll wear and I'll find you a bonnet to match. As a minister's wife you'll need to look put together when you're traveling, because you may be going to some special occasion."

The closer it came to nightfall, the more nervous Candice became. She felt awkward spending her wedding night in the Duncans' home, for some reason. Would Lucas want to spend the night together or wait until they got home? As soon as she had the thought, she realized how silly it was.

But as it worked out, just before time to go to bed Lucas and Candice found themselves alone in the living room. Candice could tell Lucas was a little nervous, too.

He came to her and wrapped his arms around her and pulled her close. "I've been waiting for this night for a while," he whispered in her ear. "But never in my wildest desires could I have imagined it would turn out like this.

"I won't be able to sleep much tonight, just knowing I have the freedom to make love with you, but I won't be able to sleep at all if we're in the same bed together. So why don't we just leave the sleeping arrangements like they are and have our wedding night when we get back to the ranch? How do you feel about that?"

Before she could answer, Mr. and Mrs. Duncan came into the living room. "We've fixed the larger bedroom for y'all for tonight," Mrs. Duncan said, looking pleased. "You two feel free to go to bed as soon as you want to."

Thinking that she might die from embarrassment, Candice smiled weakly as Lucas said, "Well, since we'll be leaving at the crack of dawn in the morning, I guess we should get a head start." And he took Candice's hand and led her toward the door of the living room, calling, "Good night!"

Mr. and Mrs. Duncan's "good nights" followed them down the hallway to their assigned bedroom.

Lucas quietly closed the door to the room. A warm glow flooded the room from an ornate oil lamp with the wick turned low. The quilt that had been on the bed from the night before had been replaced by a beautiful cream-colored silk bedspread.

"Oh, Lucas! Look at all the trouble they've gone to. What are we going to do? This is beautiful."

"What we're going to do is not disappoint those two wonderful people out there. They'll surely know if we go to separate bedrooms. So if you're okay with it, we'll just crawl into this bed and try our best to get some sleep."

"I'm okay with that," Candice said, realizing that she really was.

Lucas left the room to give Candice some privacy in getting ready for bed. She put on a new cotton nightgown, one of three she'd bought when she and Mama Tanner went shopping. For some reason she'd saved this one and not worn it. Now she was happy that she did.

She'd just gotten into bed and pulled the cover up when Lucas came into the room.

Glancing at her, he snuffed the lamp out, and then she felt the bed sink as he sat down to take his boots off. Her heart was pounding loudly, but she could still hear him moving around, taking his clothes off. Then he slid into the bed with her.

"Can I at least hold you in my arms?" Lucas said.

"I'd like that," she answered, around the lump of emotion in her throat.

Lucas placed his long arms around her and pulled her snugly against his body. She'd been lying on her back, but she turned on her side to face him.

After her eyes adjusted to the darkness, she realized that a sliver of moonlight was shining through the curtain and resting on their bed.

"Try to sleep, if you can," he said with a gruff voice. "I don't think I'll be able to, but maybe you can. Tomorrow is going to be a long day."

They lay for a while, each knowing that the other was not asleep, and Candice could feel herself getting more anxious by the moment.

"Lucas, I keep thinking about tomorrow and the next few days. What if something happens to one of us and we die, not ever having made love? I don't want that to happen. Will you love me?"

"It would be my honor to make love to my beautiful wife," Lucas answered, taking her mouth in a deep kiss.

And quietly, gently, and ever so wonderfully, Lucas Thornton took Candice Moore to heights she'd never dreamed about. He made her feel beautiful, and she'd never felt beautiful in her life. He made her feel cherished, and she'd never understood what the word meant. He made her feel like she belonged, and other than her grandmother, nobody had ever made her feel like that.

And then they both slept.

Chapter 24

THE EASTERN SKY WAS TURNING A DIM PINK WHEN LUCAS and Candice left the Duncans' home. As they waved goodbye, Candice wondered if she'd ever see them again. If they'd planned to stay in Fort Worth, maybe she and Lucas would relocate here and she'd have a friend. But now there was no telling where she and Lucas would wind up.

Mrs. Duncan had packed three times as much food for the trip back as Mama Tanner had packed for them. "You may have to hold up somewhere, if the wrong person sees you and you need to get away. I've packed enough for three days, but it can last longer if it needs to," Mrs. Duncan had said as she hugged them goodbye.

Candice felt like a new woman this morning. Making love with Lucas had been the most wonderful experience of her life. And now, just knowing that they had a lifetime together—*please, God, let it be a long lifetime*—was such a balm to her lonely heart. She made a new commitment that she'd learn these "old" ways and would make them her ways and she would be happy.

As the world grew lighter around them, Candice glanced at Lucas and almost laughed out loud. He had on a black clergy robe and a black hat that had an almost-flat crown and a wide brim. He reminded her of pictures she'd seen of Amish people. She didn't think even Mama Tanner would recognize him.

She must have made some noise, because Lucas caught her looking at him and grinned. "Well, you and that bonnet don't look like you're about to go to a fancy ball, yourself."

They laughed so hard when they looked at each other that the horse's ears twitched.

Lucas placed his arm around Candice's shoulders and pulled her close. She looked up at him, and he took her lips in a kiss that brought back the night before. Lucas was a wonderful lover, but she wasn't so sure that she was, since she was unexperienced. He hadn't complained. Still—

"Lucas," she began hesitantly, thinking it was a stupid question, "were you pleased with me last night?"

"Whoa, boy," Lucas commanded the horse, as he pulled the buggy to the side of the road and turned to Candice with a severe twinkle in his eyes. "Do you honestly think I would have come back for seconds and thirds if I hadn't been pleased with you? I can't think of anything else this morning. In fact, I've been looking for a place that would hide this horse and buggy so I could check and see if I really am as pleased as I remember."

"Lucas Thornton!" Candice said, swatting his arm. "You will not pull this buggy over and take advantage of me in the broad open daylight!"

"Don't bet on it, woman," he said, pulling her into his arms and kissing her until she felt faint.

On second thought, she might not be totally against being taken advantage of in broad open daylight.

He was about to end the kiss when they heard horse hooves pounding the ground. He kept his head down and continued kissing her as two horsemen passed them, going the opposite direction. One of them whistled and hooted as they passed.

And so their day went. They talked, laughed, flirted, and

enjoyed getting to know each other.

Lucas found it amusing that Candice would argue with him if he broached a subject she disagreed with. He discovered that he liked having a woman with a mind of her own.

Candice discovered that she loved the fact that Lucas didn't feel challenged if she argued with him. He was strong enough to let a woman be his equal. She was surprised at that, since even many men in the future didn't like to think a woman was equal to them. It seemed she'd found a rare jewel in Lucas Thornton.

They pulled off the road and found a shady spot beside a creek to have lunch. After they'd finished their meal, they lay back on the blanket Lucas had spread out. A gentle breeze was blowing and Candice could have taken a nap, but Lucas had other things on his mind as he started slowly unbuttoning Candice's dress bodice.

"Oh, no you don't," she said, sitting up and moving away from him.

"Woman, you're not supposed to deprive your man when he needs some loving," he said, reaching for her.

"Well, I'm depriving both of us. We have to keep moving. I won't get caught out here making out with a man of the cloth!" She started gathering up the food basket and blanket.

"You're a difficult woman," Lucas said, joining her in the cleanup.

"You just wait until we get home and into your bed and see how difficult you think I am."

"You've just given me something to look forward to for the rest of my day. And I will hold you to that promise."

"I didn't exactly promise—"

"Yep. You promised me a fun time in the bed tonight, and that's what I'm holding you to," he said, helping her climb back into the buggy and swatting her behind as she stepped up.

THEY MADE GOOD TIME without any problems until just before dark, when they noticed the horse's ears perk up and twitch.

"He hears someone coming," Lucas said, and immediately pulled the buggy to the side of the road. "Pray with me, Candice," he said, taking her hands in his and lowering his head as if in prayer. She did the same thing as the horse and rider approached at a high speed, slowed down to a walk and then to a stop, right beside them.

"Who are you and what are you doing with the Thornton ranch horse and buggy? What have you done with Lucas?"

"Johnny?" Lucas said, raising his head.

"Well, for crying out loud," Johnny said. "Lucas, you look plain ridiculous. And Candice, I must say that's not the best look I've seen on you, either." He burst out laughing.

"Were you looking for us?" Lucas asked.

"Yes. Mama Tanner wanted me to ride out and see if I could head you off before you got too close to the ranch. She's sure someone's hanging around watching the place. You know how Mama Tanner can get about things like that, and most of the time, she's right.

"There's a full moon tonight, so she wants you to go to the cabin and wait until after midnight. She thinks the moon won't be as bright after midnight."

"Okay. That sounds like a good plan," Lucas said.

"See you tomorrow," Johnny said, and turned his horse and raced back the way he'd come.

"Since we're only about five miles from Dallas, I think we'll find a place to pull off the road and wait until dark, just in case we meet someone else on the road," Lucas said.

"What about the barn where we stopped on our way to Fort Worth?"

"I don't think that's a good idea since Jim Hawthorne was talking about selling his place to Willard Williams. WW may have already tried to set claim to the property, and some of his men might be watching the place."

But soon he found what looked like a cattle trail that led into the tall trees, and guided the horse in that direction. The trail was just wide enough for the buggy to get through. Lucas and Candice had to dodge overhanging tree limbs that swiped at them.

Fairly soon they came to an opening with a huge pasture with cattle grazing contentedly beside a stream.

Glancing around, Lucas said, "This is more open than I'd like, but since the sun's down and it's almost dark, I don't think anyone will be riding the fence lines. So we'll just wait here for a little while until it gets good and dark, then head on.

"We'll stop at the cabin, like Mama Tanner suggested, and rest until almost dawn, then we'll walk on to the house.

"We might even find a way to amuse ourselves when we get to the cabin," Lucas added, wrapping his arms around Candice and pulling her close for a kiss.

Chapter 26

A HUGE FULL MOON WAS JUST PEEKING OVER THE EASTERN horizon as Lucas guided the horse off the main road and to the cabin. The cabin couldn't be seen from the main road, so anyone who discovered them would have to be looking on purpose or accidentally come upon the cabin.

"Perfect timing," he said in a hushed voice, stepping down from the wagon and walking around to help Candice down. "I'll unhook the horse from the buggy and tie him to a tree over in that grassy spot, so he can graze if he's hungry. Then we can go inside the cabin and rest. I know you're tired from this long day's ride."

"Lucas? Are we just going into that dark cabin without knowing if it has wild animals or spiders in it?" Candice said, just above a whisper. As of one mind they'd automatically kept their voices down, in case someone was hanging around and watching the ranch.

Lucas pulled her close and said, "I have a lantern in the cabin that I'll light just long enough for us to make sure there aren't any creatures hanging around in there. Because I don't want anything interrupting what I have in mind for us."

The chuckle that rumbled low in his chest sent chills of

excitement up Candice's spine.

"Lucas! We can't take a chance of being caught in a compromising position."

"Hey! That's the kind of the excuse you used by the creek earlier today, then you promised me a good time tonight. Well, it's tonight, so you have to fulfill your promise."

Candice could tell he was smiling, and could almost see the twinkle in his blue eyes. Well, if he was brave enough to take the chance, she sure was.

LUCAS LAY BESIDE CANDICE with one arm around her and watched as a silver streak of moonlight shone through the window and rested on her as she contentedly slept. Would he ever get tired of this woman who had come to him from out of the blue? Would he ever get used to her sassiness and her beauty?

They had made sweet love as soon as they checked out the cabin and blew out the lantern, and he was amazed at how much pleasure she brought to him. He could never, in his wildest dreams, have imagined that he'd wind up with someone like Candice Moore.

He wouldn't get any sleep tonight, because he needed to stay on guard in case someone did discover them at the cabin. But that was okay. He felt as if he could stay right here for the rest of his life and look at Candice in the moonlight and be contented.

Way too soon, he watched as the streak of moonlight started to fade and move its way from the cabin. He pulled Candice close and kissed her slowly awake. At her reluctant mumbles, he said, "I'm sorry, but it's time for us to try to get to the ranch house."

After taking care of their morning rituals, Lucas took her hand and guided her down a narrow path she'd never even noticed. "This is the path I always used when I'd come here and spend some time. We'll be able to get close to the back of the house before we come out of the trees. Then it'll only be a short dash to the house."

Dawn was just beginning to lighten the eastern sky when they hunkered down and hurried from the tree line to the back porch of the house.

Mama Tanner was in the kitchen cooking a big breakfast when they went in the back door.

"I figured you'd show up anytime," she said, wrapping Candice up in a warm hug, then doing the same to Lucas.

"Wash your hands and sit down. This is just about done. While I'm finishing up, tell me about your trip. Are you now man and wife?" She set a big bowl of scrambled eggs on the table, followed by a plate of bacon, biscuits and two large glasses of milk.

Between hungry bites, the two filled Mama Tanner in on the trip to Fort Worth.

"I'm glad the Duncans hadn't gone to Oklahoma yet, and you got to stay with them. They were like a second set of parents to Lucas when he was a little boy," she said, looking lovingly at Lucas.

Leaning back in his chair and patting his full stomach, Lucas said, "Okay, Mama Tanner, it's your turn to tell us what's going on."

Sitting down across the table from them, Mama Tanner said, "The day after y'all left to get married, I'd gone to the barn to get a hoe because I wanted to get my winter garden started.

"As you know, Lucas, I always carry my shotgun with me when I'm out and about, and especially when I know the boys are in the pasture riding the fence lines, like they were doing that day.

"Well, when I stepped into the barn I heard a noise, so I moved over into the shadows and listened and let my eyes adjust to the dim light inside the barn. It wasn't but just a minute before I saw Willard Williams over against the wall, and it looked like he was trying to set fire to the hay. I yelled at him to stop, and he shot at me."

Lucas and Candice both gasped in surprise, but Mama Tanner continued.

"So I grabbed up my shotgun and shot back at him, thinking I'd just scare him off, but I hit him.

"I yelled a few times, but nobody heard me. So I made my way toward him, ready to shoot again if he moved, but he didn't. There was blood everywhere on the floor, and I was about to try and get help when I heard men's voices and they were coming into the barn.

"I ducked behind some stacked bales of hay and listened. It was WW's men, and they said he was dead.

"Lucas, they started talking about how you'd shot him, and how they had to find you and hang you before the sheriff found you and tried to give you a trial.

"I went back to the house and waited until Johnny and the boys came in from work, and they were saying everyone in Dallas was talking about how you'd killed Willard Williams. Most folks are real happy about it, but some aren't, of course. The sheriff was organizing a posse to look for you, and WW's men were trying to find you before the sheriff did. He rode out here yesterday and asked me where you were, but I told him that you'd gone somewhere to look at a prize bull and I didn't know when you'd be back.

"I thought about confessing, but I knew the sheriff wouldn't believe a woman had actually killed WW, so I sent Johnny to look for you. Thank God he found you when he did.

"I saw a couple of WW's men sneaking around the place yesterday, and I know they're lying in wait for you."

Footsteps coming in the back door brought Mama Tanner's voice to a stop, and had Lucas reaching for his gun.

"Thank goodness you're here," Johnny said, coming into the room. "What're we going to do, boss? You can't just sit here and wait for them to come after you. They'll hang you from one of your own trees."

"What we're going to do, Johnny, is to throw them off course for a little while. I want you and the boys to come on and eat breakfast, just like you always do. Do any of the others know that we're back from Fort Worth?"

"No. Most of them don't even know where you went," Johnny answered.

"Okay, Candice and I will disappear while you all eat, then I want you to send the new hire, Carlos, into town to tell a few key people that Candice and I went to Fort Worth to get married.

"I'm thinking the sheriff and his posse and most of WW's men will head in that direction, and that'll give us time to come up with a plan.

"Send Roy to the cabin to get the horse that's tied up there, and tell him to bring the horse through the gate over on the east side of the cemetery. That way, nobody should see him with it. But even if they do, they won't think anything about a cowboy riding a horse," Lucas instructed. "Just leave the buggy there for now."

"Great idea, boss," Johnny said, heading back out the door.

"Mama Tanner, Candice and I are going to try to get a quick nap while the boys are eating breakfast. Call us when the coast is clear."

"Sure thing," Mama Tanner said, as Candice and Lucas stood to leave the room.

"Oh, and Mama Tanner," Lucas turned back to her. "Thank you for killing that son of a bitch."

"My pleasure, Lucas. My pleasure," Mama Tanner said with a huge smile on her face.

"I've been wanting to do that for years," she added after they'd left the room. "Ever since my precious daughter was killed trying to get away from him after he'd tried to rape her."

And she went about making breakfast for a bunch of hungry cowboys, feeling as if justice had finally been served to the spawn of the devil himself.

Chapter 27

CANDICE FELT STRANGE LYING BESIDE LUCAS IN HIS BED. He'd fallen asleep as soon as his head had touched his pillow. She'd closed her eyes and tried to go to sleep, but sleep wouldn't come to her. Maybe because she'd been able to sleep in the cabin for a while.

She listened as the kitchen noises slowly quieted down, and heard a horse leaving the ranch. She figured it was Carlos, heading to Dallas to spread the word like Lucas had told him to do.

Glancing at the clock on Lucas's chest of drawers, she saw an hour and a half had passed since they'd come into the room to rest. Lucas had pulled her close to him and kissed her soundly, then fallen asleep almost immediately, with his arm around her waist.

Very slowly, Candice lifted his arm and rested it on the bed beside him, then ever so gently, she slid off the bed. Since she couldn't sleep, she'd go and talk with Mama Tanner, and let Lucas get a little more sleep.

Mama Tanner was sitting at the table sipping on a cup of coffee when Candice walked into the room.

"Is Lucas still sleeping?" Mama Tanner asked.

"Yes, but I couldn't go to sleep. I slept a little while at the cabin after we got there last night," Candice said.

"Good. I've been wanting to talk with you alone, anyway. Grab a cup of coffee and sit with me.

"Have you told him yet?" Mama Tanner asked as soon as Candice had sat down with her coffee.

"Told him what?" Candice asked.

"That you're a Traveler?" Mama Tanner said.

"Mama Tanner! You know? How long have you known?"

"Oh, child, I've known from the day I saw you on the front porch," Mama Tanner said with a chuckle.

"Then the 'ghost thing' was just an act?" Candice couldn't believe what she was hearing.

"Most of it was. You did give me a momentary fright when I first saw you, because you looked so much like the Johnston woman in the pictures who sold this house to the Thorntons. But as soon as I settled down and paid attention to your clothes, I realized you were from the other time."

"But what do you know about the other time period's clothes?" Candice asked, more puzzled than ever.

"I'm from there, Candice. But more than that, I'm what's known with most Travelers as a Slider."

"A Slider?"

"Yes, I can go back and forth to any time I want to. I still have a few old family members in the modern Dallas area, and I go back a few times each year and visit with them."

"Do they know where you come back to when you leave?"

"No. I just tell them I work on a ranch far away and that it's too far for them to travel," Mama Tanner said, laughing at her own joke.

"But if you can go back and forth, you could have helped me get back home as soon as I got here," Candice said, disappointed that the woman hadn't helped her get home—until she remembered that she wouldn't be married to Lucas if Mama Tanner had helped her go home.

"I almost did, but then I saw how Lucas kept looking at you, and it dawned on me that you may have been sent to us to help out with the whole Willard Williams thing. So I talked with Dr. Wilson about it, and he suggested that I just leave everything alone and see how you and Lucas hit it off. He reminded me that I could always show you the way home if you were really unhappy."

"So you know about Dr. Wilson, too," Candice said, still trying to process all she was hearing.

"Yes, Dr. Wilson and I became aware of our situation after my daughter wrecked her buggy and lay on her deathbed for two days. I watched him doctor her, and I just knew he had more knowledge than the average doctor of this time, so I asked him.

"He told me how many times he'd gone back to the cemetery to look for the portal, so I asked him if he wanted to go back. By then he'd married his wife from here, and didn't want to leave.

"But I knew when I saw you close to the portal at Gramma's funeral that you'd found it and that you'd go back if you wanted to. I also knew that by then you and Lucas were in love, and I prayed that you wouldn't go back. I was so happy when you agreed to marry him.

"I think I have the answer to our problem, but we need to get Lucas up so I can discuss this with both of you at the same time. So why don't you go wake him up?"

When Candice opened the door to the bedroom, Lucas was sitting on the side of the bed, holding his head in his hands.

"Lucas?" Candice called quietly.

"Oh, Candice. What are we going to do now? I can't let them believe that Mama Tanner killed WW. They wouldn't believe me in the first place, but I just couldn't take the chance that they might believe me. She's the closest thing to a mom I've had, other than Mrs. Duncan, since my mom left. What am I going to do?"

"Mama Tanner thinks she has a plan that will work," Candice said. "That's why I came to wake you up. She's waiting in the dining room with a fresh pot of coffee."

Taking his hand, Candice walked down the hallway to the dining room to join Mama Tanner.

After setting a cup of coffee in front of Lucas, Mama Tanner turned to Candice. "You tell him your story first, then I'll tell mine and explain my plan, which will work if you two agree."

So, sitting down and taking Lucas's hand in hers, Candice told how she came to be on the Thornton ranch. As she talked Lucas occasionally interrupted her to ask a question, then let her continue as the look of disbelief on his face grew by the moment.

"So I'd decided I loved you too much to go back there and leave you here. I want to be your wife, no matter what our situation is. And no matter where I have to live to do it," Candice said, ending her story.

"So you found the portal back to your home, but didn't go through because you love me and wanted to stay here?" Lucas asked, even in more disbelief.

"Yes, Lucas. I'll make whatever sacrifices I have to, to be Mrs. Lucas Thornton."

Lucas leaned over and took Candice's lips in a deep kiss, not caring that Mama Tanner was watching.

"And Lucas," Mama Tanner said after Lucas came up for breath, "There's more. Do you remember me waking you up at night sometimes and taking you on a trip?"

"I thought I'd dreamed that," Lucas said with renewed amazement on his face.

"No, that actually happened. You see, your mom was a Traveler who came here just like Candice. And just like you two, your mom and dad fell in love. But your mom didn't want to stay. She missed the other way of life too much. She wanted to go back and take your dad with her, after she finally found out that I knew the way back.

"But he refused to leave his mom—your grandmother—to run the ranch by herself. So your mother agreed to marry him and try to make it work.

"She became pregnant with you right after they got married, and she loved you so much that for a while she forgot about going back. Almost. But she just couldn't get used to the hard life here. And it was a lot harder here then than it is even now.

"She began to pine away so much that your father grew worried she was going to die. So your dad agreed to go back with your mom, to try to save her life. But his requirements were that you'd be left with your grandmother, because he was afraid that taking you from her would be too much on her heart, which had started acting up by then.

"And the other part of the bargain was that I would bring you to visit them at regular intervals and leave you for a few days, then go back for you.

"That worked out for a while, but the last time I took you for a visit I found out they'd been killed in a tornado a week earlier. That's why the visits stopped."

"I used to remember those visits and all the marvelous things I saw there, and just thought they were wonderful dreams about my parents," Lucas said in wonderment. "I thought I missed them so much I was either dreaming or hallucinating."

"So, here's my plan," Mama Tanner said. "If you don't like it, just say so, and we can try to come up with something else.

"Tonight, when it gets dark, we can go to the cemetery and cross back into the modern Dallas, and stay until we see how this all works out here. Chances are that since WW is dead the bank will go under different management, and they may leave the ranch in your name. I can come back here occasionally and visit with some of my friends, and check things out."

"Mama Tanner! That's a great idea," Candice said. "I have

my grandmother's house, and she left me quite a good sum of money that we could live on. We can all live at my house. It's a big house, so there's plenty of room."

Candice looked from Lucas to Mama Tanner. Mama Tanner looked hopeful, but Lucas's face had turned a little pale.

"Lucas, do you need time to think about this?" Candice asked.

"No. I'd like to go and learn where my mother grew up, and where my dad lived when they were alive.

"Candice, if you loved me enough to stay in my land, then I know I love you enough to go to yours. And if we don't like it, as Mama Tanner suggested, we can come back here and start over."

"Or," Candice said, feeling suddenly jubilant, "We can be Sliders like Mama Tanner, and just travel back and forth when we want to. We can have two homes if we want to."

Lucas wrapped his arms around Candice and pulled her close. "Will you continue to amaze me, whichever time period we live in?" he asked.

"I promise you I'll do my best," she answered.

"Then let's get out of here," he said.

Chapter 28

A MONTH HAD PASSED SINCE CANDICE, LUCAS AND MAMA Tanner had passed through the portal back into the twenty-first century.

When they came through the portal Candice had gone directly to her grandmother's grave and knelt down to briefly visit, with the plan to come back later when she could share her adventure with Grandma. But she was so busy watching to see how Lucas was reacting to being in the cemetery that was so close to his ranch, yet so different than the one in his era, that she couldn't concentrate on Grandma.

She did take time to say, "Grandma, remember how I used to tell you that I was born at the wrong time? Well, I just took a trip to the right time and found a wonderful man. I'm married now, Grandma, and I know you'd be happy to know that, and you'd love Lucas. I'll be back later and explain."

When she'd joined the other two, Mama Tanner was showing Lucas his parents' graves.

Candice could see Lucas was fighting his emotions at seeing the graves of his parents, whom he'd thought were lost to him forever.

"You just take your time, Lucas," Mama Tanner had said.

"We'll be over here looking at other graves. Just join us when you're ready."

Then Candice had taken Mama Tanner and introduced her to Grandma. They drifted around to other graves, but soon Lucas joined them. He put his arm around Candice and drew her close. She could tell by his red eyes that he'd shed some tears, but had recovered.

"Are you two ready to go check out my house?" she'd asked. "We can come back here and visit again any time you want to."

She'd led them down the now-familiar road from the cemetery, and was surprised, even delighted, to find her car sitting where she'd left it. She'd felt sure it would have been towed. But it was a small church on a fairly unused road, so maybe someone just hadn't paid that much attention to her car.

Getting Lucas into the car was another story. Thankfully it was a large, older Lincoln, which had enough room for Lucas's long legs to fit into, so that wasn't the problem.

The problem had been just getting Lucas to get into it. Mama Tanner had immediately crawled into the back seat, indicating that she was, indeed, familiar with the modern transportation, but Lucas just stood and stared at the "contraption," as he'd called it.

Finally, he'd trusted Candice and Mama Tanner enough to get in. Candice tried to drive slow enough to not frighten him too much. She even turned on her hazard flashers, so nobody would hit her from behind. But even going thirty miles an hour was so much faster than he'd ever traveled that he held on to whatever he could find and sat, trancelike, until she pulled up into the driveway of her home.

Mama Tanner spent a couple of nights, then went on to visit with family who lived in the area.

It hadn't taken long for Lucas to learn to appreciate modern conveniences. Especially the bathroom. More especially, the shower. At first his showers were way too long, and Candice started to worry about the water bill. Then she introduced him to making love in the shower. Big mistake! He really took to that.

This morning Candice sat at the dining room table drinking her first cup of coffee while she waited for Lucas to come downstairs for breakfast. She would never have dreamed she'd miss the ranch and the lifestyle of 1875. But she did miss it. While she loved being back to modern-day conveniences, she didn't love the hustle and bustle of modern-day Dallas. She longed for quiet.

Last week Mama Tanner had taken a trip back to the ranch, and came back with good news. Johnny had told her that Dr. Wilson's father-in-law, Harold Simms, had bought the bank, and had asked Johnny to tell Lucas, when he saw him, that he'd written the ranch off as "paid in full." It seemed that Harold had been close friends with Lucas's father, and had known how hard he and Lucas had worked to save the ranch.

Mama Tanner had explained to Johnny that Lucas and Candice had gone away and that she couldn't tell him where, but they were safe. She promised him Lucas would be in touch.

Lucas had decided to give the ranch to Johnny. He'd been with the ranch for years and had helped keep it running. The one stipulation was that Lucas, Candice and Mama Tanner could visit the ranch whenever they wanted to. Mama Tanner had taken the news to Johnny a couple of days later.

But while going back for a visit seemed good to Candice, it just wasn't enough. This morning she'd had an idea she wanted to run past Lucas, and was excited to hear him finally coming down the stairs.

"Good morning, sleepy head," she teased, as he came to her and gave her a kiss.

"It's your fault," he said. "You kept me up half the night with your needs."

"Okay, we won't even talk about whose needs kept us awake.

Sit down and eat and listen to an idea I have."

After she'd gotten his food on the table, she sat down. "I've been thinking that I really miss the ranch. And if I miss it, you must be really missing that lifestyle, even though you haven't said a word. Am I correct?"

"I don't want to disappoint you, but I really do miss it."

"So why don't we sell this house and buy a ranch of our own with the money? I'm sure we can find something we can afford. That way you could continue to be a rancher." She saw his eyes immediately light up.

"But I hate to see you sell your grandmother's home," he said.

"But you gave your grandmother's home away," she argued. "Let's just look and see if we can find something, okay?"

"Are you sure, Candice? I don't want you doing that just for me."

"I'm doing it for both of us," she said.

Candice immediately started searching the *Dallas Morning News* every day, and going on the internet, looking for ranches for sale. Everything was either more expensive than they could afford, even with the sale of the house and the savings Grandma had left her, or something else was wrong. But she refused to give up. She knew there was a ranch out there somewhere for them.

In the meantime, Mama Tanner decided to slide back into 1875. She left their house at eight o'clock one night. By nine o'clock she was back.

Candice and Lucas were sitting in the living room watching TV—a very fascinating item for Lucas—when someone knocked on the door. Glancing at Candice, Lucas went to the door and opened it to Mama Tanner, who rushed in.

"It's closed!" she exclaimed. "The portal is closed! I can't get through it. It's like it was never there!" She plopped down on the sofa and stared into space, lost as to what this could mean.

Candice and Lucas were trying to process their own thoughts when Mama Tanner said, "That's it! We don't need it anymore. That chapter of our lives is finished.

"Candice was sent to us, Lucas, to help us cross the bridge back here. We don't have any more loved ones there, so there's no need to go back."

"Lucas, how do you feel about not being able to go back?" Candice asked.

"Remember, I'm wanted for murder there. I don't know how long it would have taken for me to be able to go back, anyway. Besides, as Mama Tanner said, everything I love is sitting right here in this room with me. You and Mama Tanner. I'm content to learn to live in this strange place."

A FEW DAYS LATER, Candice found a ranch that was going to be sold at auction.

"Lucas, look at this! A one hundred acre ranch with a fixer-upper house that'll be auctioned off this coming Saturday. I think we should try to get it. It's about ten miles outside of Dallas."

"What's a fixer-upper?" Lucas asked, looking confused.

"It's a house that needs work, but is still okay enough that it can be fixed up. If we get the ranch cheap enough, we may have enough money left over to fix the house."

"Then let's try it," he said.

During the rest of the week, Candice did research and found out that the house had been the estate of a last living owner and had stood empty for the past ten years. It had been put on auction twice before and two different people had tried to buy it, but both parties had run into red-tape problems and their loans didn't go through.

Saturday, when Lucas and Candice showed up for the auction, they were the only people there to put a bid down. They offered the base bid price that was requested and got the ranch sight unseen for less than the savings Grandma had left Candice.

Sunday morning Candice and Lucas asked Mama Tanner if she'd like to ride with them to check out the ranch that would soon be theirs, and they were on their way.

"This is the road to the church and cemetery," Candice said as she turned onto the road that the Google directions had given her. "I've never been past the church, so I don't know how much farther it'll be, but according to my map, it doesn't look like it's that much farther."

"There's the church and cemetery," Lucas said.

"Okay, we're supposed to look for Lamb Lane, according to the directions," Candice said.

"There it is on the left," Lucas said, pointing at a small sign.

"Johnny's last name is Lamb, isn't it, Lucas?" Mama Tanner asked from the back seat. "It's so sad to think we'll never see him again. I just can't believe the portal that I've traveled all these years is closed. I just don't understand it."

"Yes, Johnny's last name is Lamb. Maybe he has some relatives who lived in this area," Lucas offered.

As Candice turned into the narrow lane and followed it, she began to have a great sense of déjà vu. She didn't remember ever having come to this place, but she couldn't shake the feeling.

Open pasture land surrounded them for miles. Was this part of the one hundred acres that made up their ranch? Excited chills ran all over Candice, just thinking about being a ranch owner.

"Stop the car!" Lucas suddenly demanded.

Candice immediately pulled over. "Lucas? Are you okay?"

"I'm just feeling so strange," he said as he got out of the car, followed by Candice and Mama Tanner.

"I'm feeling the same way," Candice and Mama Tanner said at the same time.

An old split rail fence line ran along each side of the lane. It looked like it'd been there for decades.

Lucas walked over and ran his fingers along some of the rails that crisscrossed to make the fence. "These look like the ones the boys and I used to make the fence on our ranch. I guess in a hundred years ours will look the same way.

Suddenly Candice felt weak in the knees as a different kind of chill ran over her. "Well, let's get back in the car and go see what the house looks like," she said, trying to sound casual. Because she already knew what the house would look like.

After driving a few more minutes, the house came into view. It looked basically the same, except the weeds had grown up in the yard and around the house.

"What the hell?" Lucas said as Candice pulled to a stop and they all got out of the car.

"I think that was your fence line, Lucas. I think we've just bought back your ranch, and my Great Aunt Lela's house. Only it's a hundred and forty one years later."

"That's why I can't go back through the portal," Mama Tanner said. "Our time exchange has stopped so you two can carry on and make your own history together."

"I don't understand," Lucas said.

"I don't either, but let's see if we can go inside and find some answers," Candice said, moving toward the front porch steps that she'd walked up for the first time only months before.

She used the key the banker had given them once the contract had been signed, and opened the front door.

Cobwebs, dust and a closed-up, musky odor greeted the three as they stepped into the living room. The ladder back rocking chair and straight chairs were still there. The couch and other rockers had been replaced, but the furniture was still old.

Spotting framed pictures on the mantel, Candice made her way to look at them. Through the heavy layer of dust she could tell that the Thornton photos were all still there, along with the one of Great Aunt Lela. But more pictures had been added. Taking a tissue out of her pants pocket, Candice picked up one of the newer photos and wiped the dust off.

"Lucas, come here, please," she called. "Look at this." She held out the picture with a trembling hand.

Even though it was an older version of him, they recognized Johnny Lamb.

Lucas clutched the framed picture to his chest and let the tears flow. "He grew old in the house," Lucas said. "He kept the house and grew old here."

"There's more," Candice said, handing him a photo of a younger Johnny standing beside his bride. Apparently he'd married Mary Beth Williams.

They found other pictures of Johnny and Mary Beth in which she was holding a baby boy. Older photos showed a young man who looked a lot like his father, Johnny.

Mama Tanner had wandered away from them to do her own exploring. "Y'all come here!" she shouted from the kitchen.

The wooden table and chairs from 1875 were still there. But somewhere along the way the kitchen had been renovated with a gas stove, a refrigerator, and more modern cabinets.

"Just look at this. It looks the same, but different," Mama Tanner said, clapping her hands together.

"Mama Tanner, you know that you have to live with Lucas and me here at the ranch, don't you? It just won't seem right to be here without you."

"Well, you don't have to ask me twice about that," Mama Tanner said. "You'll need help when all the babies start to get here, anyway."

"We already need help, Mama Tanner," Lucas spoke up. "Have you tasted Candice's cooking? I mean, she can cook a good breakfast, but—"

"Lucas Thornton," Candice said, swatting him on the shoulder, "how dare you make fun of my cooking! But he's right," she added, turning to Mama Tanner. "We desperately need you here to do the cooking and all the other wonderful things you can do so much better than I can."

Then, turning to Lucas, she said, "Oh, Lucas! We're going to have the best of both worlds."

Epilogue

A YEAR LATER, CANDICE STOOD AND WATCHED LUCAS TRY-ing to saddle-break a young stallion he'd just bought from a neighbor. She jiggled the three-month-old baby boy in her arms as she watched.

The baby started fussing because he was hungry. "I've got to take Johnny in and feed him," she said. "It's time for his nap. Mama Tanner said lunch would be ready soon."

"I'll be there in a little while, but y'all don't wait on me."

Candice blew him a kiss and a smile as she walked back to the house, knowing he probably wouldn't be in until dinnertime. He was still in awe that he'd actually bought his own ranch all these years later, and spent as much time as he could working it.

After a good bit of research into the archives they found that Johnny had married Mary Beth and had one child—a son they'd named Lucas. They'd both lived to be close to a hundred years old, and had died within two years of each other in the late 1930s. Candice and Lucas had searched the cemetery until they'd found their graves in a far corner.

Johnny and Mary Beth's son had lived in the house until he died at the age of 99 in 1976. He'd left the house to his son, who'd died ten years ago. The house had stood empty since then.

Overall, repairs on the house hadn't been that extensive, and hadn't taken very long to do. Each owner had taken good care of the house.

Candice walked up onto the front porch and remembered her first time to sit there and wonder what she was going to do. That seemed like such a short time ago, and yet such a long time ago.

It just proved to Candice that time is actually irrelevant. All that matters is how you spend the time you have.

About the Author

PAT BALLARD LIVES IN NASHVILLE, TN. SHE WRITES motivational romance novels to show that plus-size women can be just as sexy, romantic and exciting as their slim sisters. Visit Pat on the web at http://www.patballard.com.

LOOK FOR HER OTHER BOOKS published by Pearlsong Press— *Dangerous Curves Ahead: Short Stories, Wanted: One Groom, Nobody's Perfect, His Brother's Child, A Worthy Heir, Abigail's Revenge, The Best Man, Dangerous Love, Adam & Evelyn*, & the novella *ASAP Nanny*—in trade paperback or ebook at your favorite online bookstore, as well as at www.pearlsong.com.

THE QUEEN OF RUBENESQUE ROMANCES also reigns in nonfiction! *10 Steps to Loving Your Body (No Matter What Size You Are)* has been called "your body's best friend in pocket form" and has been named one of the Top 100 Best Self-Help Books of All Time by Self-help.fm. It's available in trade paperback and ebook editions. Her other nonfiction work, *Something to Think About: Reflections on Life, Family, Body Image & Other Weighty Matters by the Queen of Rubenesque Romances*, is available as a Kindle ebook.

About Pearlsong Press

PEARLSONG PRESS IS AN INDEPENDENT PUBLISHING COM-
PANY dedicated to providing books and resources that entertain
while expanding perspectives on the self and the world. The company was founded by Peggy Elam, Ph.D., a psychologist and journal-
ist, in 2003.

We encourage you to enjoy other Pearlsong Press books, which
you can purchase at www.pearlsong.com or your favorite bookstore.
Keep up with us through our blog at www.pearlsongpress.com as we
promote health and happiness at every size.

FICTION

Heretics: A Love Story & The Singing of Swans—
novels about the divine feminine by Mary Saracino

Judith—an historical novel by Leslie Moïse

Fatropolis—a paranormal adventure by Tracey L. Thompson

*The Falstaff Vampire Files, Bride of the Living Dead, Larger Than
Death, Large Target, At Large & A Ton of Trouble*—
paranormal adventure, romantic comedy &
Josephine Fuller mysteries by Lynne Murray

The Season of Lost Children—a novel by Karen Blomain

Fallen Embers & Blowing Embers—Books 1 & 2 of
The Embers Series, paranormal romance by Lauri J Owen

The Program & The Fat Lady Sings—suspense & young adult novels
by Charlie Lovett

Syd Arthur—a novel by Ellen Frankel

Measure By Measure—a romantic romp with the fabulously fat
by Rebecca Fox & William Sherman

FatLand & FatLand: The Early Days—Books 1 & 2 of
The FatLand Trilogy by Frannie Zellman

ROMANCE NOVELS & SHORT STORIES FEATURING BIG BEAUTIFUL HEROINES
by Pat Ballard, the Queen of Rubenesque Romances:

*Adam & Evelyn | ASAP Nanny | Dangerous Love
The Best Man | Abigail's Revenge | Wanted: One Groom*

Nobody's Perfect | *His Brother's Child* | *A Worthy Heir*
Dangerous Curves Ahead: Short Stories
by Rebecca Brock—*The Giving Season*
& by Judy Bagshaw—*Kiss Me, Nate!* & *At Long Last, Love*

NONFICTION
Soul Mothers' Wisdom: Seven Insights for the Single Mother
by Bette J. Freedson
Acceptable Prejudice? Fat, Rhetoric & Social Justice
& *Talking Fat: Health vs. Persuasion in the War on Our Bodies*
by Lonie McMichael, Ph.D.
Hiking the Pack Line: Moving from Grief to a Joyful Life
by Bonnie Shapbell
A Life Interrupted: Living with Brain Injury by Louise Mathewson
ExtraOrdinary: An End of Life Story Without End
by Michele Tamaren & Michael Wittner
Love is the Thread: A Knitting Friendship by Leslie Moïse
Fat Poets Speak: Voices of the Fat Poets' Society & *Fat Poets Speak 2:*
Living and Loving Fatly—Frannie Zellman, Ed.
Ten Steps to Loving Your Body (No Matter What Size You Are)
by Pat Ballard
Something to Think About: Reflections on Life, Family, Body Image
& Other Weighty Matters by the Queen of Rubenesque Romances
by Pat Ballard
Beyond Measure: A Memoir About Short Stature & Inner Growth
by Ellen Frankel
Taking Up Space: How Eating Well & Exercising Regularly Changed
My Life by Pattie Thomas, Ph.D. with Carl Wilkerson, M.B.A.
(foreword by Paul Campos, author of *The Obesity Myth*)
Off Kilter: A Woman's Journey to Peace with Scoliosis, Her Mother &
Her Polish Heritage—a memoir by Linda C. Wisniewski
Unconventional Means: The Dream Down Under—a spiritual
travelogue by Anne Richardson Williams
Splendid Seniors: Great Lives, Great Deeds—inspirational
biographies by Jack Adler

HEALING THE WORLD ONE BOOK AT A TIME

www.ingramcontent.com/pod-product-compliance
Lightning Source LLC
Chambersburg PA
CBHW020652260626
47157CB00008B/3006